RanVan
the Defender

Diana Wieler

A Groundwood Book
Douglas & McIntyre
Toronto/Vancouver

The publisher gratefully acknowledges the assistance of
the Ontario Arts Council and the Canada Council.

Canadian Cataloguing in Publication Data

Wieler, Diana J. (Diana Jean), 1961-
   RanVan the Defender

ISBN 0-88899-184-3

I. Title

PS8595.I44R36 1993   jC813'.54   C93-093505-5
PZ7.W54Ra 1993

Groundwood Books / Douglas & McIntyre
585 Bloor Street West
Toronto, Ontario M6G 1K5

Design by Michael Solomon
Typesetting by Compeer Typographic Services
Limited, Toronto
Printed and bound in Canada

For Shelley Tanaka,
a gifted editor and valued friend.

Also by
Diana Wieler

Last Chance Summer
Bad Boy

ONE

RHAN was running. He had given up all hope of defending himself and now he was just moving, a flat-out, desperate dash for safety. He knew they were gaining but he was on familiar ground. He didn't have to think, only react.

Jump. Land. Watch your head! Up the stairs. Careful — jump again! Turn, turn. Hurry, stupid. Okay, clear stretch. Go! Go! Go!

Right over the rampart.

Rhan stared numbly at the screen as he fell to his death. Then he hammered the console with his fist.

Darryl lifted his head from the comic he was reading. "Again? Geez, you're having a bad night."

Rhan watched Stormers sign off and return to its pre-game mode, a taunting little clip from the easy first level.

"I wasn't playing for real. I was experimenting," he said irritably. "There's a difference."

"Sure. I make fifty cents on one and half a buck on the other," a voice called cheerfully from the front counter. "Experiment all you want."

That was Filje, who owned the store, and the game. Originally from Manila, Fil was plump and dark and sleek. He reminded Rhan of a seal. His store, the Rite Shop, sold a little of everything: groceries, hardware, incredibly ugly ceramics. But it was the games that brought in regular money. The games, and other things.

Rhan was thinking about those other things right now. Leaving Darryl, he wandered to the front and leaned on the counter.

"So what's the price today?" Rhan said.

"Same as yesterday. Fifty cents each or three for a buck."

Rhan whistled. "Too much. Jesus, how can you sleep at night?"

"But they're king size," Fil said. He took the open pack from under the counter and shook out three cigarettes.

"Don't sell to him, Fil, he's a minor," Darryl called out, without looking up. "He's wasting his money and ruining his health."

Fil shrugged. "What does he want from me? I been robbed seven times."

"The guy's got to make a living," Rhan called over his shoulder. "He's been robbed seven times."

"It's illegal, Fil," Darryl continued, singsong. "They're gonna shut you down."

Rhan sighed. "Okay, give me three and a Mars Bar."

He sauntered back and stuffed the chocolate bar into Darryl's top jacket pocket.

"You know, if you just had a little willpower, you wouldn't have to bribe your friends," Darryl said happily, unwrapping the bar.

"And one day the White Sugar Police are going to show up at your door and *then* we'll talk about willpower," Rhan said with a grin.

Rhan Van was fifteen years old, old enough to have figured out what to say when people asked him stupid questions about his name.

"It's like run, only later."

"All the designer names were taken."

"I was named after the cab driver."

None of it was true, but he liked the bewildered looks he got. And he liked his name. Rhan Van. It sounded like a cymbal, twice.

And he'd learned to say it loud. When you were short, Rhan told Darryl, you had to speak up. This summer, though, he'd noticed things. His T-shirts suddenly felt tight at the neck and armpits. And the corners of his wallet had worn two holes through the back pocket of his jeans. It surprised and buoyed him. He might not be taller, but he was certainly better packed.

He had navy eyes and silver-rimmed glasses. His dark hair touched his shoulders in back and tumbled over his eyes in front, rock 'n' roll hair that he washed and shook and let dry as it fell.

Rhan lit his cigarette and settled himself on the high stool in front of the game, waiting for the score ratings to come up. Stormers was a tracker. Players could enter a personal code and the game displayed the top scores. There were only six spaces. Most guys used their initials or a code name.

Except me, he thought. He'd had to drop a letter and squeeze it together, but he'd gotten it all in.

He grinned at the screen. His last week's high score was still at the top.

RanVan — 1,366,040.

"Well, what do you expect?" Darryl said suddenly, a breath of chocolate beside his left ear. "Nobody pumps more money into this thing."

"Oh, is that all it takes? Well, here." Rhan dug two quarters out of his pocket. "I'll buy your ride. Come on, beat me."

Darryl shook his head, stepping back. "Forget it. The thing's rigged. And the graphics are terrible. Jesus, Rhan, why do you even play this one?"

Rhan released the coins and hit start, his eyes fastening in on the screen again. "I don't know. Maybe I'm a sucker for a lost cause."

And it did seem that way. In principle, Stormers was simple. His futuristic video knight had to fight his way into a castle one turret at a time, dodging the variety of goons that came at him. If he made it to the twelfth turret, he got the girl, and another game. Simple — and impossible. He'd been playing since June and had never gotten beyond the eighth turret.

It wasn't that the opposition was so tough, Rhan thought. It was that his hero was so ill-equipped. One lousy laser! You might as well fend off missiles with a knife.

And there was no way to get more power, no extra lives to collect and blow. Your money bought you three chances and that was it.

At first Rhan thought of his hero as especially noble, braving impossible odds for the sake of a pretty face. Like a true knight, he got by on his wits and speed, not weapons.

After a while he began to think of his hero as especially *stupid* for taking on something he couldn't possibly win. And the princess — that bag should learn to save her own life. He began running off cliffs or into blow torches for spite.

4

For two weeks in August he gave up Stormers altogether and took his money to the arcade. Ran-Van was retired. The bloody machine could blow up for all he cared. But he couldn't seem to find a game difficult enough, no prize worth winning. By the end of summer he'd drifted back to the Rite Shop, to Stormers.

So the odds were stacked, Rhan thought. So the graphics were kind of stiff. So what. He liked this knight — a little bit noble, a little bit stupid — and he liked this frustrating game he couldn't win. It just felt *right*, somehow.

The lights on the screen moved in their familiar patterns. Rhan's arms felt like an extension of the machine. He knew the early levels pretty well, and he let himself slide into the rhythm.

A flash seemed to catch in his left eye. When Rhan glanced out the plate-glass window, he saw that a silver car had pulled up to the stop sign outside the store. It struck him as odd. The sleek import was a long way from home in this neighbourhood.

Just then, his knight took a direct hit. He jumped on the controls again.

Get on it or lose it, he muttered to himself.

But when he looked again, the car was still there, idling soundlessly, glowing like a phantom under the streetlamp. Darryl was watching it now, and Rhan felt a tightening between his ribs. There was no reason for this car to sit where it was.

Fil knew it, too. The veteran of seven robberies came out from behind the counter for a better look. "Better kill yourself quick," he said to Rhan,

5

his eyes on the car. "I'm closing right now."

But in the next instant, the passenger door of the car shot open and someone tumbled out hands first onto the pavement. Black jacket, black pants, short black hair. With a jolt Rhan realized it was a girl.

He didn't think about what happened next. One moment he was in the store and the next he was out on the sidewalk. The girl had pulled herself up and was leaning on the open door, swearing at the driver. She reached in and grabbed her purse, which opened and spilled over the pavement, an explosion of cosmetics and paper. She gave a cry of alarm and stepped back. The driver seized the moment and squealed away, door hanging open. Both Rhan and the girl stared after it.

When she turned back, she noticed him for the first time.

"What are *you* looking at?" she demanded.

Did she mean him? Rhan glanced over his shoulder, and saw Darryl and Fil at the window — inside the store.

"Are you okay?" he blurted, starting toward her.

"Get away from me! Get away from my stuff!"

He stopped, his hands open helplessly at his sides. When she was satisfied he wasn't moving, she dropped to her knees and began cramming the bits and pieces back into her purse.

Rhan stared. She was a bit taller than he was, and the parts that weren't hidden by her enormous leather jacket were narrow and angular. Her face was framed by thick oriental hair. What he could see was cut straight across her fore-head. It was a doll's haircut, a strange contrast to her black-lined, grown-up eyes.

His muscles felt coiled. He knew he should be doing something but he didn't know what.

"HCB 135," he said.

"What?" The girl looked up.

"That was the licence number. In case you need it."

She didn't answer, but bent to her work again. A breeze caught a piece of paper and Rhan stooped to pick it up. On it was a hastily scrawled note: *943.0843 Nazi Wives, Underground Spies.* The listing for a library book? he wondered. But then he realized she was glaring at him.

"Do you want me to call the cops or something?" he said. "Or I could get you a cab, or —"

She slung her purse roughly over her shoulder and stood up. Her eyeliner was a dark smudge at the edges of her eyes.

"Your concern is touching," she said, "but white bourgeois charity makes me want to puke."

Rhan blinked. *"What?"*

She made to stride past him, but he held out the scrap. She snatched it away, taking care not to touch him, and started down the street, her purse banging against her thigh. She looked stiff enough to break.

Rhan took a few steps after her. "You *sure* you're okay?" he called.

She whirled around and whipped up her fist at him. Sign language that needed no translation.

As soon as she was out of direct sight, the door

to the Rite Shop opened and Darryl crept out. Together he and Rhan watched as the girl became smaller and smaller in the distance, until she was only a dark ripple in the dark night.

"What was *that* all about?" Darryl finally asked.

Rhan drew in a breath, and seemed to catch a trace of perfume she'd left in the air.

"Some princesses," he explained, "are especially hard to save."

TWO

THE alarm clock blared. Rhan reached over the side of the mattress and groped for it. Bare floor. He fumbled in the crevice between the mattress and the wall for his second line of attack, a lacrosse stick to hook the cord and drag the clock over. Nothing. Gran was getting smart.

Rhan got up and shuffled to the far wall where the clock sat on the floor. He brought his bare foot down on the snooze bar, not nicely.

"Nobody tells me what to do, buddy," he muttered. He lay down on the carpet in his underwear.

Ten minutes later Gran opened the door, slamming into his thigh. Rhan rolled over, swearing.

"What's the matter with you?" she said. "And watch your dirty mouth."

"You broke my freakin' leg," Rhan said, rubbing it.

"That's not all I'm going to break. Get up for school. We're not having another year like last year, mister."

She closed the door with a thud. For a minute Rhan just lay on his back, his arms stretched out in a T. Then he started looking for his glasses.

Gran was in the bathroom when he wandered out. There was an open package of cigarettes on the coffee table and he lit one, dropping onto the couch for the first dizzying rush. The rust-red curtains were pulled but they didn't quite fit the window. The blue smoke curled and billowed into the slat of sunlight.

Rhan lived with his grandmother in a square grey building at the end of the block, across from the Rite Shop. After the row of old-fashioned two-storeys, it looked like a flat layer cake, without icing. It had been built as a post office in the 1930s, and now it was divided into six small dwellings, one- and two-bedroom boxes that had no hallways. You stepped from the kitchen into the living-room, from the living-room into the bedroom. Whenever Rhan dreamed of the house he would build one day, he dreamed of miles of hallways.

Gran came out of the bathroom. She strode over and snapped up her cigarettes.

"You can support your own bad habits, if you don't mind."

"I hate sneaking around behind your back," Rhan said, grinning.

"Sneak around. It's good for the soul."

Gran was a big woman, five-foot-nine in her stockings. Her hair had turned grey at sixteen, silver at nineteen, and now it flew out around her head in an unruly halo. She looked like Einstein, if she looked like anybody.

"You want me to write a note for your teacher?" Gran asked.

"What for?"

"So they'll let you into the boys' bathroom. You're going to run into trouble with that hairdo of yours."

Rhan threw a sofa pillow at her while she cackled. Then he stubbed out the cigarette and went for a shower.

It was a small metal stall, and when the water was on the noise was deafening. Like standing in a metal coffin while they rivetted it shut. But it was as good as headphones if you wanted to be alone. He let the steam heat the tiny cubicle and then stepped into the water and clamour.

Today it starts, Rhan thought. Last Friday was only a test-drive. Here's your map, here are your classes, get your books. It didn't count. Now it was Monday and grade ten was full speed ahead.

He'd been thinking about Bedford High since spring, and even more over the summer. He'd walked past the big sandstone building a dozen times, trying to imagine what a place looked like where you could put 1,200 kids — 1,200 strangers who didn't know who he was.

Last year everybody knew him. They didn't all *like* him, but they knew him. He was the kid who didn't turn in the assignments but passed the tests.

"Pressure," he explained to a grim-faced Gran. "I can't work unless it counts. Why show up if it doesn't really mean anything?"

"Well, ninety percent of life is just showing up," she retorted. "You get your butt into a classroom or I'll burn down that arcade myself."

But she was wrong. It wasn't the arcade, not then. Before Stormers, he'd never been hooked on a game. His problem was lunch hours that spilled over into the afternoon; his problem was Shadowfax.

Shadowfax was a shop owned by a woman named Peg, and it sold every flavour of fantasy: books, games, tapes. But the highlight of the store was the wall of comics, eight feet high and forty feet long. "The best damn selection in the city," Peg boasted.

She was probably right. The wall had everything, from the classic caped crusaders to the fly-by-night single editions — a smorgasbord of good and evil, power and pain.

"Only two kinds of people go to the wall," Peg said. "The collectors, and the junkies."

Darryl was a collector. He could spend hours studying the covers through the plastic casings, boring Rhan with his knowledge of the differences in ink technique. Peg admitted she was a super-hero junkie.

"Never could get enough," she said. "That's why I opened the store. All my Barbies were Batman — never mind the boobs."

Rhan didn't know what drew him to the wall. Sure, he liked the art and he could get into the storylines. There was a kind of camp to it all, overblown and fun.

But if you really looked, Rhan thought. If you looked beyond the powers and the villains and the plots to take over the universe. There was just a guy. Somebody who was alone, who'd been cut off from other people by disaster or birth. There was just a guy who wanted so bad to make things right.

And he understood that better than anything else.

•

Bang! Bang! Bang!

"Are you drowning in there?" Gran called

through the bathroom door. "The hydro's going to go through the roof!"

•

Rhan and Darryl were lost at sea, buffetted by wave after wave of kids. He would have argued that nobody would even try to fit 1,200 students into Bedford's tiny auditorium, if he wasn't part of the crush. Students filled the floor and lapped up at the walls, and still more poured in.

Through the maze of heads and shoulders, Rhan could just make out the little grey man on the stage at the front, gripping the microphone.

"If everybody would just sit down, we'll get through this as quickly as possible."

The crowd swirled on and on, the noise rising, the room growing stuffier by the moment. The little man tapped his microphone and tried again.

"Is this thing on? I said please, sit down! We'll do this as fast as we can!"

But it was another ten minutes before the mob had settled, and by then the grey man was positively pink from exertion.

"To those returning and those who join us for the first time — welcome to Bedford High!"

A low booing swept up from the crowd. Sitting beside Darryl on the floor, hemmed in on all sides, Rhan didn't feel particularly welcome.

"Now I realize there are more of us here than anyone ever expected. Ours is a growing community —"

He was lost in the second wave of sound, low and unhappy like a seismic rumble. Somebody,

Rhan thought, wasn't thrilled about the growing community.

"—and we're just going to have to get along!" The man broke over them, finally. "We're just going to have to do the best we can and be responsible citizens! There will be no froshing at this school, I repeat, no froshing! Such behaviour will be dealt with immediately and severely!"

The ship was lost, Rhan thought, looking at the small figure clinging to the microphone. The man was sailing in stormy seas and the slightest nudge of wind would sweep him onto the rocks.

Rhan gave up and glanced beside him. Darryl was drawing, his notebook open on his knees, a black-and-white reality coming to life under his pen. It wasn't just what he drew, but how. No pencil, no eraser; the fluid black lines flowed onto the paper in deft, easy strokes.

As if it was all finished in his head, Rhan thought. As if it was just the thing of getting it down.

Darryl could draw anything, but he was best at ancient warriors poised for battle, or superheros tearing a streak across the sky. Bulging muscles and gleaming metal; mythic beasts and vile villains, not to mention big-breasted women falling out of their clothes. Rhan didn't know much about art, but he knew what he liked.

This time Darryl was drawing one of their own creations. Over the blue lines of looseleaf, Arachnaman took shape, complete with his trademark complex vision — eight eyes — and deadly fangs that were a real obstacle on a date. They had come up with Arachnaman last year during lunch hours, and he seemed to be the one Darryl brought to life when he was feeling really low. Arachnaman was so hideous he always cheered them up.

Now Arachnaman was poised, but still. Rhan pulled out a pencil and scrawled the thought balloon.

Trapped! Humans on every side, and with the blood lust rising within me! No — no, must not succumb. Only my arch enemy, Fly Specks, could have engineered this tortuous fate. Wait, isn't that him, up at the microphone?

Darryl's hand flew. In brilliant strokes he created an enormous fly in front of a podium, lecturing.

I must end it now! In the name of Justice, Fly Specks must be stopped! But how to get through this crowd of humans — without stopping for a snack?

Arachnaman leapt — he was a jumping spider — over the crowd and onto the stage. Darryl flipped the page in his binder and in moments Arachnaman had Fly Specks cornered.

Nitey-Nite, Specks! It's time for the Big Sleep!

That's what you think, Anachra-nism! You never suspected my secret weapon!

The hero faltered, aghast.

Oh, no, it's...it's...

"RAID!" Darryl and Rhan chorused out loud. Every head within a thirty-foot radius turned to look. Darryl shrank and Rhan's face burned, but he stubbornly kept his head up. Moments later a buzzer sounded, saving them all.

Rhan got up, relieved to stretch, to move again, but he wasn't in any hurry to leave. The kids who had entered as a steady stream now rushed for the exit as a mob, pandemonium that Fly Specks didn't even try to stop. Rhan hung back, a little dazed from the heat and noise and his sudden U-turn back into reality.

Then, something in the crowd caught his eye. Blue-black hair, thick and glossy, but short. Very short. Rhan felt a leap inside. He turned to his friend.

"Hey —"

"No," Darryl cut him off. "It's not her."

Rhan looked again, but the doll's haircut had disappeared into the crowd.

•

"The key to the whole thing is not to use the map," Rhan said.

"Right," Darryl said.

"That's how they know you," Rhan said. "They're looking for guys looking at their maps. You open that sucker and the next thing you're walking down the hall painted green or somebody's flushing your head in the john."

"Right," Darryl said. "How do we find the cafeteria?"

Rhan glanced left and right, then leaned deep into his open locker and opened his map. After a second or two he pulled out, shoving the paper in his pocket, closing the door with his foot. He started confidently down the hallway, Darryl at his heels.

"You got it?" Darryl whispered. "You know the way?"

"Nope, it was too dark. Couldn't see a damn thing."

"Maybe we should check..." Regular meals were crucial to Darryl.

"I'll starve first," Rhan said.

He had only been in grade ten for one morning and he already knew the most important thing was not to look like a grade ten. By the second class, he'd seen a rash of kids with "I'm a Baby Bear" written in magic marker on the back of their shirts — courtesy of the Bedford Bears football team. One poor soul was crawling around with "Goldilocks" on his shirt. Cries of "Oooh, baby, who's been sleeping in *your* bed?" followed him everywhere he went.

Rhan liked his shirt just the way it was. And he wasn't anybody's baby bear. He resolved to keep it that way or die in the attempt.

In his own opinion, he thought he looked like a grade twelve, or an eleven at least. He knew how to swagger down the middle of the hallway.

"It's the walk," he told Darryl as they searched for the cafeteria. "You have to look like you know where you're going, even if you don't."

His friend studied him for a moment. "Oh, you've got the walk," he said. "It's the *height* that's missing."

Darryl needed coaching, Rhan decided. He was big enough to pass for a grade twelve, but he kept drifting toward the edge of the hallway, close to the lockers. When anyone glanced at them, Darryl looked away. That was just the way he was; it had been the same in junior high.

Except now it mattered, Rhan thought. It was survival. He was going to have to work on Darryl.

By 12:36 they still hadn't found the cafeteria. Darryl couldn't stand it anymore and started toward the school store, which housed two junk vending machines, along with a popcorn counter.

"Forced into a Mars Bar," Darryl said, grinning. "Tragic. I'll have to choke it down somehow."

"Your problem is that you don't have enough faith in me," Rhan grumbled. "I mean, I'll find it sooner or later."

"That's what worries me." Darryl started backing away. "Next week is 'later,' too."

"You know, loyal sidekicks used to be a whole lot more...*loyal*," Rhan called after him. Darryl waved cheerfully.

By now Rhan was craving his own vice. He wanted a smoke. He had one he'd stolen from Gran on his way out the door this morning. There wasn't time to get out to the school courtyard before the one o'clock bell, but he knew another place.

Rhan was an expert on smoking in school johns: where and when and how not to get caught. On his tour last Friday he'd seen a three-star facility — the boys' room off the gym. Connected to the locker room, it had its own entrance in a small, secluded hallway. Perfect, but he had to hurry.

Zipping through the network of corridors, he noticed the cafeteria sign, and grinned to himself. Tomorrow Darryl was going to get a lesson in faith.

There was more movement now, kids beginning to trudge back into the school. Weaving through the flow he missed his turn and had to go back. But then he got it right and strode down the little hall with a surge of satisfaction. What a memory. He had his hand on the door when a noise made him look back.

They were bearing down on him, a solid wall of bodies, shoulder to shoulder in the narrow hall. He registered five faces the same instant the realization shot through his body: this was a dead-end corridor.

Get through the bathroom, into the locker room. Just make it to the gym. Someone will be there. Christ, somebody had to be there!

But they were moving fast, so fast that one of them wasn't touching the ground. Rhan stared. The middle kid was skimming the polished floor, rigid and pale, carried along in the grip of the guy on either side.

Suddenly they were towering over him. The tallest one looked down into his face.

"You don't want to go in there," he said.

Rhan backed away so fast he stumbled. They swept their passenger into the bathroom, a knife through water. The door eased slowly shut.

For a moment he just looked at it, dizzy with relief. God, that was close. It would have been four on one.

Then, sounds. Muddled words he couldn't quite make out. Vibrations in the floor, a panicky shuffle, and thunder. It was still four on one.

Rhan reached for the door handle, a bare twitch

before his hand fell away.

You don't want to go in there.

But he did. Face on fire, throat so tight he could barely breathe, he could have torn the door off its hinges, just to end the wanting to do it.

But he couldn't.

"How brave you are now."

He whipped around. The girl from last night was standing in the mouth of the corridor.

He'd been right, she did go to Bedford, but it was still a shock. Fluorescent light was not street light. Without her high-collared coat he really saw her now, the black mop of hair cut level with her eyelashes, everything shaved beneath. She looked supernatural, elfin. Someone Darryl might have drawn.

Except she was blocking his only way out. That was real enough. And she had seen everything.

"There's four of them," he blurted.

"Nobody's telling you to beat them up."

"They saw me. They know who I am." He started toward her, putting distance between himself and the bathroom door. "And I don't even know the guy."

"You didn't know me, either, but that didn't stop you. Tell me, *blue eyes*, do you save all your good will for minority groups?"

A tightening pain. He glanced over his shoulder at the door, then back again.

"Look, this isn't my problem —"

"Not yet." She cut him off. "But some day it might be, and then you'd better pray the guy on the other side of the door has some *guts*."

She turned on her heel, turned her back on him again. The fury was on his tongue like a hot pepper. Rhan dashed up to where the corridor met the hallway. But when he saw her slight, sinewy body folding into the crowd, nothing came out. He watched her leave for the second time, helplessly staring at the back of her bare, bare neck.

THREE

OSMIC cockroaches, that's what they were. Running like vermin into holes and cracks. RanVan took careful aim.

Bzzt! Bzzt! Bzzt!

Safe on his precipice, he slew them as they ran, fired into their retreating backs with a deep and satisfying pleasure.

Bzzt! Bzzt!

Oh, wait. Missed one.

Great and Powerful Lord! I beg you to spare me, not for myself, but for my family. I throw myself at your feet and plead for mercy —

Eat neutron, pig. Bzztt!

RanVan was in a murderous snit. He knew he should be moving on to the next level — time was running out — but he stayed to slaughter. RanVan the Merciless. RanVan the Blackhearted.

Bzzt! Bzzt! This was really fun.

Actually, he had abandoned unnecessary brutality early in his gaming career; it slowed his pace. It was also a waste of energy. In Stormers, you got the most points for *where* you got to, not who you blew away.

But tonight he wasn't playing to win. He was playing for vengeance.

Even Fil noticed the difference.

"What are you up to? Doesn't sound right." He wandered by to watch, but when he saw what Rhan was doing, he became alarmed.

"What're you shooting for? Come on, you got to get out!"

The next instant, though, Rhan's knight blipped and vanished. Out of time.

Fil shook his head. "Suicide. You know better."

"It's my money," Rhan said stubbornly.

The storekeeper leaned against the ice cream freezer.

"School?" he asked.

"Worse."

"Women?"

Such a funny, grown-up word. And the plural yet. Rhan grinned faintly.

"Ahhh," Fil sighed. "Hey, you want my advice?"

"No."

"Well, you're gonna get it. Listen." Fil lowered his voice. "Women are trouble. You want a woman, what happens? You sleep with her, maybe marry her. Then kids. What happens? They need braces. Pfft! Your life, it's over. You're working to pay some dentist. Women are trouble."

Rhan laughed out loud. Good old Fil.

"So *there* you are!"

Rhan turned. Gran was standing in the doorway of the store, hands on her hips, water dripping off her plastic rain hat.

"Everybody's got to be somewhere," Rhan said.

"Well, *this* somebody had better get his behind over to Suite C. That rug's got to be finished tonight. We got people moving in tomorrow at nine sharp."

Rhan sighed. "You know, you'd get better service if you weren't so cheap. I just can't get excited about minimum wage."

"How excited can you get about broken bones?"

"Fil, call the cops! This is child abduction with the threat of violence!" Rhan cried as she tugged him firmly toward the door.

"Good night, people, good night." With a chuckle, Filje waved them away.

Into the rain. They hurried over the puddles on the pavement, and at the curb, Gran stuck out her elbow. "Here. Help a little old lady cross the street."

"Sure," Rhan said. "Point her out."

It was an old joke. In his mind, Rhan was sure Gran could have carried *him* across piggyback. But when he took her offered arm, he was uneasily surprised. Even through her raincoat, she felt different. Not frail — Gran could never be frail — but looser, somehow.

How old was she, anyway? he wondered. It was another big joke around the house. Gran always said she was thirty-nine, but now when he tried, he didn't even know what decade to put her in. Fifty? Sixty? Seventy? He was suddenly angry. What if he had to know this sometime? She could get hit by a bus and go into a coma and there he'd be, her only relative, and he couldn't even tell them how old she was. What if she was old enough —

Rhan stopped. Suite C had no curtains and the light from the window struck him like a beacon. He was suddenly aware he was still hanging onto Gran's arm and he pulled away, self-conscious.

"Hurry up," he said, with more snap than he meant. "I'm getting soaked."

Gran was fumbling through the ring of keys. "Well, hold your horses, and get out of my light."

She unlocked the door and he followed her in. After the darkness and drizzle, the room seemed uncommonly bright, almost yellow. Or maybe it just smelled yellow. He saw Gran's cleaning supplies and disinfectants next to the wall, but the odour of cat pee almost knocked him over. For all her work, this suite still had a long way to go.

If the building had a caretaker, Gran was it. She took applications and filled the vacancies and called the police if the parties got too wild. She delivered the evictions and cleaned the suites. And even Rhan, who was only in charge of carpets, knew that if you had to evict somebody, you were going to hate cleaning the suite.

Tonight, though, he didn't really mind — not that he would have admitted it. It felt good to be an expert at something. This wasn't some wimpy, user-friendly rug steamer that you rented from the grocery store. It was an industrial carpet cleaner — old, complicated and downright cantankerous.

But he could handle it. He had a year's experience under his belt, and with a length of wire and a roll of duct tape he could clean any clog or bandage any break in the old hose. He was the Master of the Rug and he could handle this baby in his sleep.

It was a good thing. As he pushed the heavy equipment around, wrapped up in its vibrating roar, he felt himself drifting. He couldn't stop thinking about the girl. Not how she was today, blocking the way, pinning him with her eyes, but how she was last night. Over and over he saw her tumble, until he could almost feel the pavement scrape his own hands.

Who was she? Who had thrown her out of the car, and why? He thought about the title he'd seen on the scrap of paper: *Nazi Wives, Underground Spies*. No one he knew would check a book like that out of the library. It made him want to find it, and read it.

By ten o'clock the Master of the Rug was sticky with sweat and his right shoulder ached. It was time for a break. Gran had her head in the oven, scrubbing and muttering, and he swiped a cigarette from her pack on his way to the door.

When he pulled it open, a stomach was blocking the way. Rhan stepped back. He knew this stomach. Usually in business suits, it was dressed for a nightclub now — expensive leather jacket and gold at an open collar. A paunchy Romeo.

But this was not a romantic visit.

"Out," the landlord said. "I want to talk to the old woman."

Rhan scraped his back on the doorframe as he squeezed around him. But it was either that or touch him. He jumped the stairs and started down the sidewalk when he heard a voice behind him.

"And keep your grubhooks off the car."

Rhan whipped around in time for the slam.

"My crowbar's in the shop," he said to the door.

The air was fresh and cool. It would have been nice if it weren't for the miserable drizzle. Rhan knew he could have stayed dry by huddling on the steps — there was a small overhang of roof — but he refused. At this moment he preferred misery. He lit his cigarette and sauntered toward the white Eldorado.

They didn't make cars like this anymore, they didn't dare. You couldn't justify this bloated thing, almost fifteen feet long and fully three thousand pounds. It had been built before unleaded gasoline, before pollution controls, before people *knew* there was an environment.

It ought to be in a museum, Rhan thought, shaking his head. It had to cost a fortune to keep on the road. But he knew why the landlord kept it. Even now, it was a great white presence that others would have to swerve around to get past. It was a bully of a car, even when it was parked.

He had always hated this man, but it seemed worse tonight. How he looked, how he sounded.

"I want to talk to the old woman."

Gran would be horrified to be caught like that — hair in curlers, covered in grease — but it was beneath Eldorado to call first. He came when he came, and everybody did what they were told.

Even me, Rhan thought bitterly. He watched the pools gather on the big white hood, gather and swell and run down the grill. If only he had that crowbar, or something.

Rhan fingered the side mirror. Skimpy thing for such a boat. Held on by a bit of chrome. One kick, one hard kick, and it'd go flying. In his mind's eye he saw it shatter gloriously on the pavement.

His heart was pounding. He backed away, two long strides.

Do it.

He leapt and kicked — beside it. He felt a rush of disappointment, and relief. That was a practice.

Rhan flicked his cigarette into a puddle and backed up again, only this time along the front end of the car. One hand on the hood would give him height, and leverage.

He deserves it, the pig. Do it!

But he was frozen, dizzy, like standing at a cliff edge.

Do it — coward.

A scraping noise behind him, metal on wood. Rhan backed away from the car in a sudden flinch. When he turned he saw the landlord easing his bulk through the doorframe.

Oh, no — what did he see?

But the man was smiling at him as he ambled over, a sly, conspirator's grin.

"Can't stay away, huh? I knew you'd be no different. The guys are always sniffing around, drooling over this baby. She's hotter than sweet sixteen on a Saturday night."

The landlord chuckled at Rhan's expression and unlocked the driver's side. But he hesitated, leaning on the open door.

"Hey, she's *better*," he said with a wink. "She doesn't cry after."

He eased himself in behind the wheel, laughing. The engine surged to life with a roar, and Rhan had to scramble to get out of the way. But after the car was gone, he stood in the road, staring after it. Oh, if only he lived in another time — if only he had a sword! The desire tingled over his skin. He would have been a defender of honour, and he knew it.

But in this time, his chance to do anything had come and gone. He dragged himself back into the suite.

Gran was leaning against a wall in the kitchen.

"I guess I'd better get on it," Rhan said, starting toward the carpet cleaner. "Or we'll never finish tonight."

"Don't bother." Gran's voice was flat.

"Why not? Isn't somebody moving in tomorrow?"

"Not anymore."

"Oh." Rhan was at a loss. "Well, at least I got a start for next time."

Gran hadn't moved. "I don't think there's going to be a next time — not for this suite," she said. "We're just supposed to lock up and give him the key."

"Why?"

"How should I know?" she snapped. "It's not our place, is it? It's none of our business. I guess he can do whatever the hell he wants with it!"

He had the feeling she'd been given the same answer, in just the same way. It made him furious.

"You're the caretaker," Rhan shot back. "You have a right to know what's going on. But everybody jumps for him — no questions asked. That's his whole problem! He struts around like King Toad because we let him think that's what he is!"

Gran moved away from the wall with a sigh.

"Talk to me in ten years, little boy," she said. "When you're putting a roof over your own head, and maybe somebody else's. You tell me who's jumping for who."

Fireball in his stomach, sudden and fierce and bright.

"I won't!" he blurted. "I'm not just anybody and I won't!"

Gran stopped. For a long moment she just looked at him, into him, a hard stare that made him feel every day of fifteen. But too much had happened today for him to back down. The girl's word seemed to reverberate in his head. Guts.

"You mean that?" Gran said finally.

"Yeah."

A faint smile stole over her face. "That's my boy," she said. "Now let's get our stuff and call it a night."

FOUR

"**I** THINK she's got the hots for you."

Darryl blushed. "Get out," he said. "She was looking at you."

"No way," Rhan said. "If she was looking at me, it would have been her right eye. That was definitely a left eye look. And deep. Definitely a deep left eye look."

Darryl grinned. "Probably something in her contact."

"Yeah — rampant female lust!"

On impulse Rhan turned to look behind him, triggering Darryl to look, too. In a flicker of eyeshadow, the tall brunette winked.

Both boys spun back and kept walking. Darryl turned scarlet. Rhan exploded.

"A left eye *wink*! What'd I tell you. Come on, killer, you got her on the line. Just reel 'er in."

"God — you!" Darryl shoved, a playful push, but it sent him staggering.

Rhan pulled himself up. Coaching, he thought, was a thankless job.

He'd been working on Darryl all week, and he'd seen a little progress. Darryl wasn't skulking along the lockers anymore, and he could talk to Rhan in a crowded hallway without whispering. But he didn't talk to anyone else. Left alone, even for a few minutes, and Darryl dove into his binder, sketching frantically. It was, Rhan thought, a safer place.

And probably a saner one. By Friday he'd had five full days of Bedford Senior High. Not long,

31

but long enough.

Bedford was a school caught by surprise. Fly Specks was right; the district was growing. Rhan himself had seen the rush of new and renovated homes sprouting up like mushrooms after the rain. But this was the first time he'd felt the crush — in classrooms so packed you had to walk sideways to your desk; in the tiny gym that turned every game into a stampede.

But there was something more. Froshing had died out in a matter of days, or at least there weren't any more "Baby Bears" walking around. But the vibration was still there. People really looked at you here, Rhan thought. Or they looked you over. What he had, what he wore. And as the days went on he realized there was a question behind the endless glances: Did you move into Bedford, or were you just born here? A Renno, or a Res? And for the first time, too, he realized that one meant money and the other didn't.

Rhan and Darryl had reached the cafeteria. Rhan had heard it called the Sacrificial Caf, and it hadn't taken long to figure out why. Meals were prepared by surly grade twelves in Food Services, who'd failed out of Computer Sciences. It was dished out by even surlier grade elevens, who were mad because they had to wear hair nets in front of their friends.

"You get your slop with a *glop*!" he told Darryl in the line-up.

What bothered him most, though, was the size of the place. Bedford had never expected to house 1,200 students, much less feed them. The lunch hour was staggered into two shifts but it didn't help. The fifteen tables could only seat twelve each.

And often they didn't. Most of the long tables were quickly taken over by small groups of kids, sometimes as few as six, and nobody else dared sit down. Darryl and Rhan and all the other lesser creatures were left waiting against the wall, holding their trays.

Darryl didn't care; he could eat standing up. Rhan didn't care if he ate; it was standing he resented.

Suddenly, though, he spotted an empty corner at the end of a table.

"Over there," he said, steering Darryl, who carried the tray with both meals. But the instant Darryl set it down, someone stood up. Tall and wiry, long brown hair, expensive sunglasses. Definitely Renno category.

"Take a hike, Jumbo. The table's taken," the Renno said.

Darryl was embarrassed, from the mistake as much as the insult, and hurriedly picked up the tray. But Rhan was right behind him.

His irritation flared. It had been a long week. He looked directly into the black reflection of the sunglasses.

"Sit down, Darryl. The spot looks free to me."

Darryl glanced apprehensively over his shoulder, but Rhan was blocking his escape.

"You got a hearing problem, fat boy?" the Renno said. "I said beat it."

Darryl picked up the tray again. Rhan grabbed

his arm. "Sit down, Darryl. You're a student here. You've got certain rights."

"You're giving yourself the right to die, butt-head." Kids nearby stopped eating and looked up.

"Rhan," Darryl pleaded quietly, miserably.

Rhan's heart was thumping under his shirt. His bravery with Gran had caught up to him. The problem with saying stuff was that you started to believe it. He wasn't just anybody — even if he was scared to death.

"Is that what you do?" he said. "You're the table police? You're devoting your life, your intelligence, to governing furniture?"

The Renno glanced to his left, grinned faintly at his friends and leaned forward on the table, making the muscles in his arms and shoulders bulge.

"And what if I am?"

"You're underqualified," Rhan said.

The Renno lunged for him and caught a handful of shirt, but Rhan wrenched himself away, dragging the other guy into Darryl's tray. It crashed to the floor. Chairs scraped in the flurry of kids moving out of the way. The Renno pulled himself upright, inhumanly fast.

You ain't gonna beat him, you ain't gonna beat him. Think or die, RanVan...

Rhan leapt up onto the table.

"There is something wrong," he shouted, "really *wrong* with a school where ten percent of the students get one hundred percent of the tables!"

The cafeteria froze. The crash had gotten their attention and now every eye was rivetted in disbe-

34

lief. Darryl's mouth hung open. The Renno stepped back, horrified to be connected — even remotely — to something this weird.

Rhan was rushing, scared and thrilled at the same time, but he felt safe on the tabletop. Just another precipice. He had been on those before.

"And there is something wrong," he shouted, "with a school that *allows* that ten percent to get away with it! That allows the other ninety percent to be terrorized every single day!"

There was a lone whoop from the wall, and then an echo. The noise released the attending Food Services teachers from their stupor. Rhan saw them moving in.

Think faster.

"So until that ninety percent gets some *guts*, this school is going to give that ten percent absolute freedom to do whatever the hell they want, one hundred percent of the time!" he screamed.

There was a roar as he was yanked to the floor. And Darryl finally sat down, his face in his hands.

•

"Please tell it to me again, Mr. Van. It is not that I disbelieve *you*, it is only that I disbelieve almost everything."

His name, Rhan had read on the doorplate, was Dr. Sahota, and English was not his first language. The soft, clipped accent sounded British, specifically *learned* British. Sahota's skin was coppery brown, and his hair was black, what was left of it. Aside from that, Rhan didn't know if he was sitting in front of the principal, the guidance counsellor

35

or the head janitor.

Rhan was perplexed. He had expected to be dragged in front of someone — probably Fly Specks — and he'd been geared up for a roaring good fight. It was unnerving to find himself sitting in this quiet office in a comfortable guest chair.

But he wasn't quite a guest.

"Mr. Van, I am breathless with anticipation."

"I was standing up for the rights of a friend," Rhan said boldly. "His right to sit at an empty space in the cafeteria. I don't think the administration of this school cares that there is an extreme shortage of tables, or that ten percent of the population has a *monopoly* —"

Sahota cut him off by lifting his hand.

"This friend," he said. "He sought your defense of his rights? He is unable to speak for himself?"

Rhan felt a flush of heat. He'd been concentrating so hard on the Renno, he'd forgotten about Darryl.

"Sometimes people are afraid to say what they think," he said.

"But obviously Mr. Van is not." It wasn't a question but Rhan could feel the expectancy. He knew what was coming next.

"Because it pisses me off," he blurted. "It pisses me off that some people can make life miserable for other people and everybody knows it and nobody does a damn thing about it!"

"I agree wholeheartedly. What is your plan?"

Rhan opened his mouth, then shut it again. Of course he didn't have a plan. He'd only gotten into this thing an hour ago.

"Do you think," Dr. Sahota said, "that a few more tables in the cafeteria would effect a change in this school? That it would stop what is happening?"

Rhan saw his chance. "And what do you think is happening?"

"You tell me, Mr. Van. I wasn't shouting in the cafeteria."

There was silence, and the man thoughtfully folded his hands on his desk. "Do not come to me with problems, come to me with answers. Think *first*, Mr. Van, and I will be happy — I will be eager — to meet with you. Civilized people solve their differences through discussion," he finished.

"I was *having* a discussion," Rhan snapped, "with two hundred other people."

Sahota was surprised; he almost laughed, but caught himself.

"Well, stand up for your rights, Mr. Van, but do not stand on our tables. Because if that is your only plan, then one day you will walk in and they will *all* be standing on tables — and you will still be short."

Rhan found himself in the hallway very suddenly. It was not, he thought, a guidance-counsellor type of goodbye.

FIVE

DARRYL was late. Rhan leaned against his own locker and waited — ten minutes, fifteen. He was puzzled, then irritated. They always met here, Darryl knew that. Every day in this bloody school they had met here and they would bloody well meet here *today*, too. He crossed his arms over his chest — and waited.

Eyes passed over him like headlights, but he met them dead on, an unflinching, iron gaze that made all the girls blush, and some of the boys. He'd had a whole afternoon of this — the sideways looks and sudden giggles, conversations that stopped when he entered a class.

It didn't touch him. He was untouchable. Because I was *right*, he thought. Sahota hadn't shaken that and these ingrates didn't shake it now.

But that was the nerve. The ingratitude. What was the matter with people? I did it for you! he wanted to say. This is the beginning, this is your chance. Rise and overcome!

They didn't rise. They didn't overcome. They stared.

Twenty minutes. Where was Darryl, anyway? He let his iron gaze slide until it was on his shoes. Just resting it, Rhan told himself. Don't want to wear out the batteries. He realized he was bone-tired. He felt he could fall into bed and sleep until Monday. Or June.

"Your motives are fine but your technique stinks."

Rhan looked up and his heart sank. Oh, great.

The last person he'd hoped to see was his self-appointed social conscience. But he'd never let her know it.

"Thanks," he said pleasantly.

"I mean, spontaneous resistance has its advantages," she went on, "like shock value, but it's kind of kamikaze. Only a martyr or an idiot doesn't plan an escape route. There's no sense fighting for something if you're not around to enjoy it."

"Oh, I don't know. I kind of have my heart set on dying for a good cause. The problem is there aren't a whole lot of them around anymore."

He saw a hint of bewilderment — and leapt for it.

"I mean, there used to be all kinds of causes to die for: the Crusades, blood feuds, beautiful women. But times are tough. I have to take what comes along. Freelance."

On a whim, he bowed.

"Rhan Van, at your service."

When he looked up, her lips were rippled in a grimace that was trying to hide a smile. He felt a surge of success. He had surprised her, finally.

"Well, freelance martyr, did they suspend you or what?" she said.

"Are you kidding?" he said breezily. "Sahota made me tea."

"That's too bad. You could have gone to the press. Then you'd really have something. There are just so many angles here: elitism, racism, overcrowding, administrative incompetence." She was talking rapidly, excitedly. "There'd be an inquiry — the press would put Sahota through the meat grinder. And it's about time. They deserve it — this school system, this whole festering neighbourhood!"

She caught herself.

"But it would seem," she continued in a flat voice, "that Sahota *defused* the incident. And judging from the crowd," she gestured at the empty hall, "you don't have much of a fan club. I guess there's a fine line between a spontaneous demonstration and a freak show."

Rhan straightened at the sudden pain.

"You showed up," he said. He turned on his heel and started down the hall. The right way, the wrong way, he didn't care.

Go home, Van. Go to sleep. Maybe you won't wake up.

"Wait!" her voice was behind him, trailing him. "Wait, I didn't mean it like that. Social revolution has to start somewhere. We needed this — really!"

He didn't answer and he didn't slow down, but she caught up anyway.

"You're a shock to the system. You do things, then you don't," she said. "It's weird. I haven't figured you out yet."

"Why even try?" he said. "Don't you have a life? Why keep barging into mine?"

"Just a minute. You barged into mine first, remember?"

Rhan snorted. "And you were pretty thrilled about it. I remember that, too. Well, what if I want to un-barge? Can't we just pretend we've never met?"

"No. Destiny isn't retractable."

It went over him like a whisper of air. Strange word, destiny. Not the kind you flipped out at people. It belonged to a different world — Shadowfax, or Stormers.

He looked at her through narrowed eyes. "Who *are* you?"

Her name was Thalie Meng and she was seventeen. Born in Vietnam, she'd left with her mother when she was four.

"The last ones on board for the Great American Guilt Trip," Thalie said. "The war had been over for five or six years then, but the U.S. was still so guilty, so embarrassed about Vietnam that all you had to do was say 'Political Refugee,' take an oath and swear you'd work for minimum wage for the rest of your life."

Hanoi to San Francisco, San Francisco to Vancouver. "The only suitable environment for my mother, 'the artist.' Oh, don't worry," she hurried on. "You've never heard of her. She's not very good."

Without ever deciding on it, they were walking together, first through the hallways and then outside. In the back of his mind he guessed he was walking her home; these weren't his streets.

He was burning to ask her about last Sunday night, about what had happened in front of the Rite Shop. Who and what and why. But the chance never came up. Their conversation turned and ran down so many avenues, some he had never been down before.

"...and they're ugly," Thalie was saying. "They're worse than ugly. They're conspicuous consumerism."

"So's the label on the pocket of your jeans," Rhan countered. "It's smaller, but just as conspicuous. It's the same thing."

"No, it's not," she retorted. "I didn't shred two other pairs of pants to get it. I didn't destroy anything."

They were talking about monster houses in Bedford. The city was growing at breakneck speed, expanding in a rush of suburbs and new development. But most people wanted to live in the city's heart, close to the ocean. For that reason, people had pounced on the little houses in old neighbourhoods like Bedford, fixing them up and selling them at a healthy profit. It was the Renno phase.

Then came something else. In mid-August Rhan had watched bulldozers flatten two houses. The roaring machines had scraped away the buildings and yards, even the fence between them. The new house went up fast: soaring beams and dramatic angles. It towered over its neighbours, so big and different it might have dropped from the sky.

It had made him feel strange. Not Renno, he thought. Rennos didn't scrape away two perfectly good sources of profit. There was something else at work here. When he heard the new name, monster, he couldn't disagree.

Right now, though, with Thalie, he found himself defending them, or at least the right to build them. There was something about this girl that made him want to argue; his tiredness had evaporated under a new fire.

"But doesn't the growth of anything depend on the destruction of something else?" Rhan said.

"They killed trees to build those old houses in the first place. They destroyed the natural habitat of something to build this school."

"What's happening now isn't growth, it's greed. Nobody wants to live next to a monster; people are complaining like crazy. But the city won't put a stop to it because they're terrified they'll piss off the new, rich immigrants."

Hong Kong money. Rhan had already heard a lot of resentful words about the influx of newcomers into Vancouver, wealthy families who were fleeing Hong Kong before the land reverted to Communist control. But Thalie's bitterness surprised him.

"You're not exactly a pioneer yourself," he started.

"I said *rich.*" She cut him off. "Let me tell you, blue eyes, your country has more than one kind of welcome."

She could stretch the air, this girl, pull it tight like a sheet across a bed. He had to shake it off.

"Well, *I'm* desperately poor," Rhan said. "No wonder you're crazy about me."

A moment's hesitation, then he thought he saw the corner of her mouth turn up, although she didn't look at him.

"But how did riff-raff like you get into Bedford High?" she said, playing along.

"Quotas," he said. "For every ten filthy rich you've got to have one filthy poor."

She laughed, sudden and light.

"Believe me, the only monster on my street is me."

Thalie shook her head, still grinning. "You're weird," she said.

He hadn't been reading the street signs, but he knew they were in Renno country. The houses had been growing as they walked. Little bungalows had stretched up into two- and three-storey homes with balconies and sunrooms. He was just beginning to wonder where Thalie lived when she stopped abruptly and turned to him.

"Well, thanks for walking with me," she said. "You have...interesting views."

"Even if you think they're all wrong?" Rhan said.

"Oh, not *all*," Thalie said, "just most." There was an awkward pause. "Well, see you around."

The message was polite but very clear. She was going the rest of the way alone. Rhan felt a tug, quick and sharp. He still wondered about last Sunday night, but he couldn't find the courage to ask.

"Yeah, sure," he said. "See you."

After half a block, he turned to look. He'd only meant to see which way she went, see if she was gone yet, but before he knew it, he was walking again. Following.

Rhan trailed a full block behind, sometimes more, making sure to stay on a side with convenient cover. Once he had to duck behind a hedge, his heart racing.

This isn't honest, Van, he told himself. She didn't want you here and you know it.

But he couldn't stop. It was like being pulled along by a string.

At an enormous yard, Thalie turned in. Up the

walk, then she unlocked the elaborate double door with her key.

Rhan wandered up slowly. It was a grand old house, and somebody knew it. Fresh paint and manicured lawn; the driveway looked like pink stone. For an artist who wasn't very good, Thalie's mother did all right — more than all right. He didn't understand. The way Thalie talked, she must have been poor at one time.

But not now.

Rhan stared. The more he found out about this girl, the less he seemed to know. And — the desire clutched at him — he did want to know. Maybe he could ask her out sometime. At school, or if he walked her home again. Maybe if they went out, they'd have more time to talk. Maybe she'd tell him...

To go to hell, Van. Think about Sunday night. She wasn't exactly crying out for help, you know. Whatever's going on with this girl, she's not telling anybody.

But he wasn't just anybody.

And while he fought with it, wrestled with it, the garage door began to rise as if by magic, and the silver car sailed past him, up onto her driveway, and inside.

•

The door was only open a hand's breadth, but it was enough to see the displeasure on the woman's face.

"Oh, it's *you*," she said.

Rhan sighed inwardly. It had been two years now, and Darryl's mother had never said his name.

But then she'd never said, "Why don't you come in?" either. It was, Darryl finally admitted, because she thought he had a smart mouth.

"Well, he isn't here," the woman continued. "It's Friday, so you know where he is."

Actually, he did — he'd just forgotten. Between Thalie's house and here he'd forgotten the day, the hour, and almost everything else.

"Yeah, all right," Rhan said, backing away. "I'll catch up with him there. Thanks."

But she didn't close the door. "Good money," she sniffed. "I can't get over it. By the time his brother David was his age, he'd finished with all that. By the time David was fifteen, he'd given up all that little boy stuff."

Rhan stopped, suddenly angry. "For what — little girl stuff?"

He saw her mouth pull into a tight line, right before she slammed the door.

Rhan spun around and started to walk. Okay, so he had a smart mouth. He also had a smart *brain* and he loathed Divine David, the Jock. Almost as much as Darryl did.

Shadows were lengthening, suppertime was coming on. Rhan picked up the pace and shrugged Darryl's mother out of his mind. He didn't have time to waste on that woman. There was someone else who needed him more.

The princess is in the tower of the Dark Lord.

Even as he thought it, he gave himself a jab.

Get real, Van. This isn't the game. You're not playing the freaking game. And anyway, you could be wrong.

But he knew he wasn't. He'd never mistake that car; he'd never forget it, silent and silver, like a whisper or a ghost. He was burning to tell somebody who'd understand.

Peg looked up when he walked in, then tilted her head toward the back of the store.

"Proceed with caution," she whispered. "He's got one bear of a mood on."

The words didn't register. Rhan charged ahead.

Darryl was at the superhero wall, in the DC section, studying. New editions came out on Fridays and the latest *New Titans* was firmly in his grip. It was always first choice: he had every edition since Grummett had taken over the pencils. But money was tight, so every other purchase was a matter of grave consideration.

"Hey, I've got to talk to you," Rhan started, but Darryl didn't budge. His eyes never left the wall.

"Are you home or what?" Rhan said irritably. "I said I've got to talk to you!"

"What makes you think I want to talk to you?" Darryl still wouldn't look at him.

"Well, *excuse* me. I thought I was talking to a friend."

"A friend wouldn't stand on a table and embarrass me to death," Darryl blurted. "He wouldn't tell everybody, 'We are grade tens, please pick on us.'"

Time warp to the cafeteria. So much had happened since lunch. He'd almost forgotten about it, but Darryl hadn't.

"So that's what's bugging you," Rhan said.

"Yeah, it's bugging me! God, I almost died. I

47

kept thinking, Why is he doing this to me?"

"Wait a minute. I was helping you. The guy was hogging the tables..."

"So what?"

"So it wasn't fair."

Darryl whirled on him. Rhan was surprised to see how red his face was, just talking about it.

"Of course it wasn't fair! But, Jesus, Rhan, we gotta live, too. We have to go there for three years. Don't you ever think about stuff like that?"

"Yeah, I do! And I know that if I let some jerk treat me like shit today he's gonna be doing it three years from now, too!"

For the first time they realized they were yelling, at each other. Abruptly, Darryl looked away.

"Well, you handle it then, but leave me out of it. Don't help me, Rhan."

The sound of his voice, like a nickel tumbling into a well. Rhan paused.

"Even if you're drowning?"

"Even if I'm drowning."

"Even if you're drowning with your mint, first-edition *Crusaders*?"

The faintest grin. "I'll toss it to you."

"Okay," Rhan said. "I'll make sure it goes to David. I know you'd want him to have it."

Whack! Darryl thumped him with *Titans*. "I'd rise up out of the grave." Whack! "I'd murder you in cold blood."

Rhan backed out of range, grinning. Darryl got mad but he always cooled off.

But the other thing hadn't cooled. In fact it was revving inside him, again.

"I think somebody we know is in trouble," he said.

Darryl lowered the comic slowly, listening while Rhan hurried over the details. He didn't mention meeting Thalie in the hallway by the gym, though, or that he'd followed her home uninvited.

"But it was the same car," Rhan said. "I'm sure of it."

"But you don't know," Darryl said uneasily.

"I'm sure!"

"Okay, you're sure. But so what? You said she had a key; nobody was forcing her in at gunpoint. This sounds like somebody who knows exactly what she's doing."

"But maybe she doesn't have a choice," Rhan insisted.

"Did she tell you that?"

Another jab, a big one. Rhan fell silent.

"Look," Darryl said patiently, "I'm not saying you're wrong. I just don't know what you want —"

"We could call on her," Rhan broke in. "We could just go to her house and see..."

"Oh, no." Darryl took a step back. "Forget it. Not in a million years."

"Why not, for Christ's sake!"

"Because I mind my own business," Darryl shot back. "Because I don't help people who don't ask for it."

"Some people never get the chance to ask." Rhan's heart was thudding in his ears. He could feel them both skirting the border of sacred ground.

Darryl lowered his voice. "Rhan, tell the cops.

Tell Guidance at Bedford. But don't get involved in this."

Rhan nodded and started backing away toward the exit.

"Okay," he said.

Darryl was clutching *Titans* nervously. "Hey, I'll call you, Sunday or something." His face, his eyes said *Don't do this*.

"Okay," Rhan said. He turned, and the wall seemed to catch him, hold him, for an instant. Then he pushed through the door.

Okay.

SIX

I T was a relief to run. Like a slingshot held back too far and too long, he was released into the night, his feet light on the pavement, his jacket flapping open.

What would he say when he got there? Who would answer the door? What if she wasn't home?

But the questions blew away as he ran. He was just going to see — he didn't have to do anything. He leapt over a bus bench without touching it.

The last few blocks he slowed, winded, but his heart was still drumming as he went up the long walk. Common sense had kicked in. God only knew what was going on in there.

Beware. The word tingled through him as he knocked.

"Yes?"

Rhan stared. She was beautiful, this woman. Six feet tall, or so it seemed, with her black, upswept hair and high forehead. She was slender but not frail, bones led into more graceful bones. Still, it was her eyes that astonished him, liquid brown, elfin — and familiar. He knew those eyes from another face.

"What can I do for you?" Her irritation jogged him back to reality.

He stuck out his hand. "How d'ya do. The name's Rhan. I'm here to see Thalie."

She looked at his unexpected hand and smiled, amused. But she shook it.

"I'm Lei Meng, Thalie's mother. Why don't you come inside?"

She moved back and he stepped into the foyer. The ceiling soared twenty feet above him, rooms opened to his left and right. A wide polished-wood staircase turned and twisted up out of sight.

It's a good thing I'm hard to impress, Rhan thought, but he stayed on the mat.

"Thalie's upstairs. She might be having a shower, but I'll check," Lei said.

When he was alone, Rhan took a breath and mustered the courage to peek into the rooms. The one on his right looked like a sitting room. Dark, delicate furniture — Chinese, he thought — and on a small table he could see a half-finished puzzle. On one wall a fireplace crackled with bright life.

The room on his left was dimmer, but more intriguing. The double French doors were open, and even though no lamps were lit, he could still make out a large humped shape. Too small for a couch, too big for anything else. It drew him closer until he was in the doorway, and then he saw that it was a sculpture — one of many. Some were waist high, some sat on tables, but all had the same smooth undulating curves. Fascinated, Rhan wandered into the room.

And then he noticed the photographs. The walls were crowded with pictures, and Rhan strained to see what they were.

Suddenly the light flicked on and he whipped around, caught.

A man was standing near the doorway, grinning.

"Hiya," he said. "How's it goin."

At first glance, he struck Rhan as a college student,

with his longish hair and jeans and shirt. Then Rhan noticed the receding hairline, faint creases in the skin around the smile. The pale brown hair looked ready to grey any minute.

"Hi," Rhan said. His thoughts were racing. Was this *the* man? The driver of the silver car? And was he mad that Rhan was in this room?

But he didn't look mad. He drifted over, pointing to the large photograph Rhan had been studying.

"That's a good one, isn't it? I took it just after dawn, on the beach. I don't know if I'll ever get that same light." He pointed out highlights in a few others, contrasts and photographic effects. Rhan could see now that they were all the same subject — Lei running, jumping, standing. The same Asian face, the same graceful body.

"You took all these?" he asked cautiously.

"Everybody needs a hobby," the man said, and he shrugged good-naturedly.

Rhan's eyes swept over the walls again, and he felt a chill. They weren't all Lei. That one, and that one, and that one. He stepped closer to the picture of a girl sitting with her arms around her knees, her hair flowing around her like a cape. Thalie was here, too, in this collection. And sometime between then and now she'd hacked off her long, shiny hair.

"You're like me, dude," the man said softly. "You know a thing of beauty when you see it."

Rhan's guts clenched. He jerked around, but at that moment Thalie burst into the room, hair wet and eyes blazing. She glared at the man, who winked at him and sauntered out. She shut the door after him and whirled on Rhan.

"What are you doing here?" she demanded. "Who said you could come here?"

Rhan was dumbstruck, but not for long. "It's nice to see you, too," he said.

"Look," Thalie said, "you just can't go sneaking up on people ..."

"So who's sneaking? I didn't come in through a window. I knocked. It's not a crime. Avon does it all the time!"

"How did you know where I live?" she asked.

"There are things called phone books, you know."

"But we're not listed, not under our name." She took a step closer. "You followed me, no, don't lie — you did! Why?"

Trapped. She wouldn't accept a lie and he wasn't quite ready to tell the truth.

"I wanted to know you," he blurted. "You... your ideas about social anarchy and...and spontaneous resistance." He grappled, trying to remember the things she'd said. "Well, it's interesting, and kind of up my alley."

Her expression didn't change, but he could feel her measuring his face with her eyes. He held his breath. Did she believe him? Did she even want to?

"Let me get my coat," she said finally.

The air was cool and damp, pure pleasure. With the big house falling away behind them and the whole night open in front of them, he felt himself surge back to life. He didn't know where they were going and he didn't care. He was on his own turf.

The whole world was his turf, except that house.

"Well, you seem to know a lot about me," Thalie said, "but I hardly know anything about you — aside from being a freelance martyr." She sounded more relaxed out here, too.

"That's easy," Rhan said. "I'm almost sixteen and women adore me. The safety of the free world rests on my shoulders, and women adore me. That doesn't leave a lot of time for a hobby."

Thalie rolled her eyes. "I mean, do you live at home?"

What a funny question. Wasn't wherever you lived "home"?

"I live with my Gran," Rhan offered.

"Where are your parents?"

"They ran away to join the circus." An old answer, smooth from years of use.

"Lucky you," she said.

She was silent then. It seemed to be the opening he'd been waiting for.

"Have you lived in Bedford a long time?" he asked.

"No."

"When did you move in?"

"Last April."

"Do you like it?"

"No."

"Does he live there?"

Dead silence. He'd slipped the question in, hoping she'd just answer it without thinking.

But she was thinking. They seemed to walk a long time with it hanging between them, like a spider's thread. He wanted to say something, take it back or make her laugh, but it was too late.

"Of course he lives there," Thalie said finally. "It's his house."

In low, flat words the story came out. The man's name was Garry, and he'd once been the Boy Wonder for a computer software company. Then he got smart and began working overtime, copyrighting his creations and selling them on the open market. Two programs hit the big time and Garry suddenly wasn't anybody's Boy anything.

"Doesn't seem fair, does it?" she said, wistfully. "Just two programs to Easy Street."

She and Lei had met Garry at a showing of her mother's work.

"Not a gallery, don't get me wrong. It was one of those basement things, the Starving Artists' Collective or something."

Only one piece sold that night — the sculpture that was too small to be a couch. But a few days later Garry went to their apartment and bought something else. And again, and again. When Lei ran out of things to sell him, they moved in.

"And he started taking pictures?" Rhan said.

Thalie looked at him sharply, then away. "And he started taking pictures," she said.

They had reached the school. Somehow he'd known they were coming here. There were lights in the courtyard, and Rhan could see dim auxiliary lights through the windows, but Bedford High itself seemed to exist within a black hole. The surrounding streets were so dark and quiet; an occasional car and the low rushing of wind through the trees.

They sat on a concrete bench against the wall that faced the parking lot. Rhan's insides were running in tight circles, like a creature in too small a cage. He wanted to do something; he wanted to show her...what? That he was somebody who could do something.

A sudden sliding of metal made them both look. Twenty paces down the sandstone a door opened and a man came out. In the bad light Rhan couldn't see his face but he had a grandfather's stoop, and his jacket and pants were distinctly uniform green.

A janitor working late, Rhan thought, faintly surprised. From outside, the school had looked deserted.

They watched him lock the door from a huge ring of keys, then tug on it to make sure. It was an old school with old doors. The janitor made his slow way to the parking lot but when he reached the car in the corner spot, he suddenly thunked his fist on the roof. He turned back toward the school.

Probably left his car keys in the staffroom, Rhan thought idly.

And then the idea crawled over him, an electric tingle. He wanted to grab Thalie's arm to tell her, but he didn't dare. He sat, barely breathing, praying she wouldn't move.

She didn't. The janitor trudged past, not even glancing in their direction. He muttered over the lock again and went inside. As soon as the metal clanged shut, Rhan was on his feet.

"Yes or no," he said.

She looked up at him, puzzled. The chance was

sliding away. He jerked his head toward the door.

"Yes or no."

Thalie smiled. And then they were sprinting along the wall.

When Rhan grabbed the handle he half expected a jolt, the pain of yanking his shoulder out, but the heavy door opened with a scrape and a faint puff of school air. Old paper. He leaned inside.

Now his heart was pounding. Now this was possible. He peered down the dim halls for movement, his ears straining. But Thalie was right behind him; he couldn't chicken out now. Rhan took a breath and went in.

He glanced around hurriedly. They had to get out of sight. But he never went out these doors, and all hallways looked the same in the dark. A distant shuffle made Thalie grab his arm.

She tugged him into a short corridor of lockers — a dead end, Rhan realized with panic. But there wasn't time to argue. They squeezed themselves into the small hollow between the lockers and the far wall — half the space of a phone booth — and waited. And listened, and waited.

He could smell the leather of her jacket, hear the softest rustle as she breathed. Her elbow was pressed into his side, a dull circle of pain, but he didn't ease away. He was frozen, his muscles knotting, his glasses sliding down his nose. He was sure he could feel his pulse where their bodies touched.

What if we get caught? he wondered. What if we don't?

It took forever for the footsteps to become loud

enough to be close; for one horrible minute there was no sound at all. Rhan closed his eyes. He could see it, the janitor standing at the mouth of the corridor, squinting at a shadow on the far wall...

The thud of the heavy door made him flinch. He stiffened again, not believing, and for seconds they still waited. It was Thalie who burst out first, and Rhan staggered after her.

"Oh...God," she gasped, limping around. "I feel I could fall over."

"Yeah," Rhan said weakly. "I have that effect on women."

Thalie hesitated, and then she laughed, full of relief.

They started to walk from one auxiliary lamp to the next. The empty school seemed like another world — familiar things stretched out of perspective by the wrong light, the wrong time. A comic-book world.

"So what's your plan?" Thalie asked.

"Plan," Rhan repeated.

"You know what I mean. You broke in to demonstrate your defiance of autocratic authority — that's obvious — but it's no good if they don't know it. You have to send them a message," she insisted.

"Should I fax it to them or leave it on their answering machine?"

"Listen, I thought this was important to you. That's how you talk. When I saw you in the cafeteria, I actually believed it."

Papercut words, right to the bone. It mattered

to him what she believed.

"Okay," he said after a moment. "I've got an idea. Come on."

After a few false starts and wrong turns, he found the cafeteria. The kitchen, with its expensive training equipment, was locked up tight with sliding doors. But in the large room where the students ate, the plywood tables and twenty-year-old chairs weren't worth stealing.

Rhan wasn't there to steal. Pushing in through the double glass doors he felt a tremor. The streetlight through a row of high windows painted the furniture ghostly grey. He took a breath and strode over to the first table, pulling the chairs away. Then he grabbed one end of the table top and looked at Thalie.

"You want to give me a hand?" he asked. "It's not heavy, just kind of awkward."

Puzzled, she took the other end. Rhan guided it over until its surface was on the floor, its legs sticking straight up like a dead animal.

"Good," he said, and moved on to the next one.

It wasn't hard work, but it was work. By the tenth one Rhan could feel the heat in his shoulders, and a trace of sweat along his hairline. But when he looked out at the growing rows of road-kill tables, he felt a gust of pride. This was a message anyone could read.

When they'd flipped over the last one, Rhan hurried over to the doors to take in the whole effect. He turned to Thalie.

"Well?"

She was slowly working her way toward him,

hands in her pockets. The heels of her flat shoes made a faint *click*, *click* in the silence.

He tried again. "Pretty dramatic, huh."

"It's nice," she said, stopping beside him. "It's fine."

Rhan was pierced. Nice? *Fine?*

"Well, don't look like that. It's just...oh, forget it." She turned away.

Rhan stepped sideways, blocking her. "No, what? Come on, it's just what?"

"I thought you were going to do something," Thalie burst out. "Don't you understand? This won't touch them. On Monday someone will turn over the tables again and that'll be it! We might as well not have even been here."

He was getting mad. "So you've got a better idea?" he demanded.

"Yes." Her dark eyes flashed. "You have to hit where it hurts, where they still have sensation. You have to cost them. The time for passive resistance is gone."

"This better idea — I still haven't heard it," he snapped.

"Then watch." And she seized a wooden chair and hurled it at the glass doors.

SEVEN

THE glass didn't break; it exploded — a sudden jagged storm on the polished floor. The heavy chair landed and skidded, coming to a stop against the wall of lockers in the hall.

Rhan stared. He expected an alarm, as if the door was wired; he expected screaming and flashing lights and the police. But there was nothing. The stillness was as perfect, as unreal as a soap bubble.

Then his reflexes kicked in. Get out, get away. He made for the door, pushed on the metal frame that was intact, and out into the hall. He was halfway down it before he realized he was alone.

Rhan turned. Thalie hadn't moved. She was still standing there, the anger gone from her face. Everything was gone.

She was crazy, she had to be. What kind of person throws a chair through a glass door and then stands there looking at it? Keep going, he told himself.

But he couldn't. He was the one who had brought her here, into the school, into the cafeteria. In a way, this was his doing.

"Hey!" he called softly. "Come on, we have to get out." No response. He took a few more steps. "Can you hear me? I said I'm going. I'm going right now!"

No answer. Under the hacked-off hair her face was a bronze sculpture. Artwork, or that girl in the photograph. That thing of beauty.

Garry's words seemed to grind through him

again, and the fury sprang up in its wake. Laser blue. It swept over his scalp like a helmet, around his arm like a shield.

I won't leave you.

Into his hand like a sword.

RanVan won't leave you behind.

She flinched when he took her arm, like someone waking up from a dream. But he pulled her firmly through the broken doors.

"We're going now," he said.

This time he led her through the dark halls and half-lit stairwells without hesitation. He was an expert at mazes. When they finally reached the parking lot door, he charged at the bar, and almost threw his shoulder out.

He swore at it, tried again, rattled it heroically, trying to shake something loose in the old mechanism.

"We're locked in," Thalie said, a frightened edge to her voice. In the back of his mind he realized he should be panicking, or at least be worried. But he was running on a rush and he just didn't have time for mortal failings. He slammed the bar once more for good measure, but the old door barely quivered.

"Okay," RanVan said, "I've got another idea."

He started in a new direction, still holding her hand. His mind was whirring back to an art class he'd had at the beginning of the week. The instructor had warned them about the metal door at the end of the hallway.

"That is a fire escape," the man had said sharply. "It's alarm wired. You sneak out for a smoke and the fire trucks will be here in just under two minutes to douse you and your cigarette."

Now RanVan found the little hallway, windowless, pitch black. He groped his way along the lockers, tugging Thalie like a reluctant pony. She didn't want to follow him, but she wasn't letting go of his hand, either.

"We can get out at the end here," he said. "It's a one-way door; it won't be locked." He measured out the smooth cylinder of the door bar with one hand and tightened his grip on Thalie with the other. His heart was pounding.

"There's a football field on the other side. Do you think you could run it in less than two minutes?"

"I don't know. Why?"

"Because you're going to have to — *now!*"

He threw his weight against the bar and it flew open. The night sky seemed brilliant after the hallway; the air was like silk against his face. In the next instant the alarm was screaming through his bones. It broke him and Thalie apart and chased them down the hill.

They ran and ran. He felt the motion as if it wasn't part of him, as if it was something he was watching, not doing. Once he managed a glance over his shoulder and saw Thalie right behind him, her mouth drawn open in a grimace, gulping air. The first wail of a siren shot them forward; they weren't out of the field yet.

They hit the sidewalk and kept going, but the pace deteriorated. A ragged gallop became a half-hearted lope, and in another block they were just staggering forward.

He was relieved to see the park. Once only a stretch of grass and trees, it had gone Renno now, too. There were new benches and a brightly coloured children's play area with slides and swings and a sprawling network of fibreglass tubes.

He led her toward a yellow tunnel and they crawled inside. It was just big enough to sit up in with their knees pulled up to their chests. The tube was easily ten feet long but they huddled in the centre, their shoulders almost touching.

For a while there was only the sound of their ragged breath, amplified by the tunnel. It was only a memory now, that laser blue feeling. He was just exhausted, and completely human.

And so was she. The tunnel was very dark, but he didn't have to see her to know how near she was. The long run had left the scent of perspiration on her: bare skin under leather on a warm day. And shampoo. She wasn't artwork; she was a living thing.

A living thing that had destroyed a door with a chair. When she touched his hand, he jumped.

"Do you think it was right?" Thalie said.

"I think what I did was right," he said carefully.

"I know you probably think I'm terrible or crazy or something." The words rushed out. "But I just feel things. And sometimes it gets so big ..."

She broke off, and he heard her take one breath, two, before she spoke again.

"I can't talk to most people. They're walking around locked in their little worlds, and they're just so *vacant*. They don't believe in anything, they wouldn't fight for anything.

"I read a book about the French Resistance, you know, during the Second World War? There were women who were part of the Resistance, but they were married to Nazi sympathizers. And they stayed married to them, because they knew they could do more damage living under the same roof, that there were other ways to fight."

That book. In his memory he held the scrap of paper again, saw her on her knees on the sidewalk, gathering up the bits from her purse.

"Do you believe in evil?" she said.

Rhan caught his breath. Like a password into a fortress, it threw open the doors and dove inside, into the place he never took people. He gripped her hand, fingers locked.

"Yes," he whispered.

"So do I," Thalie said.

And then she kissed him, hard.

•

It was late by the time Rhan walked home. When he looked at his watch he realized he was scheduled for certain death. He hadn't shown up for supper and he hadn't called, and here it was now, late. He didn't look at his watch again.

It was like being drunk. He was giddy but clear, striding along in total control — superior control — except he kept walking off the curb.

RanVan the Triumphant. RanVan the Defender. Door Finder, Night Crusader, He Who Was Possibly Maybe in Love ...

He stumbled off the curb again. A car horn

blared through his bones. He scrambled back onto the sidewalk, jackhammer heart.

Get a grip, Van, or you're going to become a legend *tonight*.

But it was hard to concentrate. His mind was a whirlwind. A sprawling palace with its mother-and-daughter beauties; a wink from the Dark Lord. Night sky and school air; the smell of leather very near his face. When he remembered the cafeteria door, he winced. He hadn't had a plan tonight, but if he had, that wouldn't have been in it.

It was still your idea, he jogged himself. You were in front every step of the way.

But I wasn't going to throw anything! I wasn't going to destroy anything.

The argument ran around and around in the same little circle, but he couldn't resolve it. It wasn't that smashing the door was wrong. Rhan could believe in wrong, he could justify it, for the right reasons. But unnecessary. He couldn't bring himself to believe in that.

Except the rest was so good! Walking now in the cool air, the night felt like a new thing. To talk to somebody who understood, even if they didn't always agree, seemed incredible. Do you believe in evil? The question still echoed through him, a miracle.

And the other parts, the parts that weren't talking, they seemed pretty miraculous, too. There were times when he'd been swept along in the sensation of it, the heat of her hands, the press of her lips, and where.

He had reached his street. At the far end of the block, the Rite Shop was still open, the light from the big front window warming a square of damp cement. The place where she had landed. The guilt turned on him in a sudden, sinking bite.

And you deserve it, he warned himself. Thalie was someone in trouble. She needed his help, and that came first.

Keep your priorities straight, RanVan. And no more broken doors.

The bell of the Rite Shop tinkled merrily as he pushed his way in. At the back of the store, stocking shelves, Fil waved.

Rhan settled himself on the high stool in front of the game. He knew he should be getting home, but late was late. A few more minutes wouldn't make a difference. And he really wanted this right now.

Deposit coin and hit start.

The familiar whirlwind as the characters fell into place, the brilliant blue armour of the under-equipped but valiant hero. Except this time the knight saluted at him.

Rhan stared, heart pounding, but the magic didn't surprise him. He knew something had happened to him as he led Thalie out of the school. Something that felt like fire and lightning and Christmas day. And for all his analyzing he hadn't looked at that moment. Any more than he'd have to look at a comet, to know he'd caught it in his hand.

EIGHT

RHAN collapsed on the couch.

"Oh, no, you don't," Gran said, bustling out of the bedroom. "You got a date with some dirty dishes, mister."

"Give...me...a...break," Rhan panted. "There's... child labour laws, you know."

Gran grabbed his left foot and yanked it off the coffee table. "Any fella who thinks he can miss supper, *without phoning*, and stay out 'til all hours doesn't qualify as a child in my books." She stood glaring at him until Rhan pulled himself up and started toward the kitchen.

"And I want 'em dried, too," she called after him. "Don't think I can't tell the difference!"

It had been a grim sort of day. Last night he'd known he was in trouble; he'd been prepared for it. But *work*. He was never prepared for that.

From the crack of dawn   well, ten o'clock, anyway — he'd been working from Gran's master list of chores, horrible, unfair things that he'd been putting off for weeks, would have put off for the rest of his life, in fact. The worst part had been cleaning the little wooden platform where the suites heaped their garbage, that and the chewing out he'd gotten from Gran. He'd caught a lot of hell in the past few years, but this time something was different.

"I'm not runnin' no hotel," she'd said finally. "You keep coming and going when you please — acting like you live alone — and believe me, you'll be doing it. But not under this roof. You think I don't mean it, just try me."

The steel in her voice stayed with him the rest of the day.

Now it was after supper and Rhan was dying to get out of the house. But he was in a dilemma. No one had actually said he was grounded, but if he asked, or tried to go out, it'd be the perfect opportunity for the subject to come up. He filled the sink and leaned in on his elbows until the suds were almost touching his nose. He was wondering if anyone had ever drowned in dishwater.

"Now that's what I call an attractive man — one in front of the sink."

Rhan twisted around. Gran had just come out of her bedroom again, wearing the first grin of the day, and her lucky shirt. He felt a rush of hope. Bingo night! He'd forgotten. If she left without saying he was grounded, he had her on a technicality.

"What are you smirking about?" she asked, walking across the room to collect her purse.

"I was thinking that if you're hot tonight, you could pick me up a Porsche on the way home."

Gran laughed ruefully. "Fella, this jackpot wouldn't buy you a Chevette. And anyway," her face seemed to tighten, "I'd put it away for a rainy day. Just in case."

She was already leaning on the door when the phone rang. Rhan's nerves yanked. He knew Darryl's ring. Gran moved to answer it so he pulled out of the sink, streaming water.

"I'll get it!" He waved her away. "You don't want to miss the early bird card!"

He waited until the instant the door shut to pick up the phone.

"Be here in ten minutes," he told Darryl. After he'd put down the receiver he leapt straight up and touched the ceiling. Sometimes, Rhan thought, life worked.

"I don't get it," Darryl grumbled as they pushed their way out of the arcade. "You were the one who wanted to go in. I never blow good money on that stuff. But we weren't there for ten minutes and then it's a big deal to leave."

"Good money," Rhan repeated irritably. "Is there such a thing as bad money? You make as much sense as your mother."

Darryl fell silent, stung, and Rhan felt a tug of conscience. He didn't mean to be mean, but the whole night had been like this: jab and dig and snap. He didn't get it, either.

His insides felt tight, overwound. After the first relief of getting outside, he'd been restless. All their usual haunts were suddenly boring, and even worse was the sensation that something was counting down the seconds, like the clock in the corner of the Stormers screen. He was running out of time, but he didn't know for what.

He couldn't stop thinking about last night, and the fact that he didn't have a plan. Usually he hated people who plotted and agonized over every detail. He was better at winging it — being in the right place at the right time. But this was different. Now it was someone else's life.

Questions were rising inside him like bubbles, things he desperately wanted to talk over with somebody. But he hadn't told Darryl about last night, and once you started not telling, Rhan thought, there was only more and more you couldn't tell.

He stopped on the sidewalk. A second later, Darryl did, too.

"What?" he said.

"That's where she lives," Rhan blurted. Without thinking it, deciding it, he had somehow drifted to the right street and now he was across the road from Thalie's house.

It didn't look quite as big at night, but more eerie. The pink stone driveway was ghostly pale. All the windows on the second storey were dark, but a few on the main floor were lit, including one on the side of the house, the one he knew was the fireplace room. He was astonished, captivated, by how well he could see in.

After a moment Darryl shrugged. "Nice place," he said and tried to keep going.

A flutter of movement in the side window. Rhan's heart skipped. That's where they were. He took a step closer, but it wasn't enough. The angle of the window and a nearby tree were blocking his view. He took another step, and another.

"Rhan..." Darryl's voice seemed far away.

Rhan turned, and realized he was standing in the middle of the road.

"Let's go," Darryl said. "Okay?" He didn't sound angry, only anxious.

"I just want to make sure she's all right," Rhan

said. He glanced back at the side window. It was eight feet off the ground. "I'm going to need your help."

Darryl started backing away. "Oh, no. Forget it. I can't."

"Jesus Christ!" Rhan was suddenly furious. "Do you always have to be such a coward? Isn't anything ever important to you?"

"It's illegal, Rhan. Don't you understand? What if we get caught?"

"I never ask you for anything," Rhan said, his breath like the beginning of a fire. "Never."

For a moment they just stood, one on the sidewalk, one in the road.

"Oh, God," Darryl finally mumbled. "All right. But just for a minute, I swear! Then I'm outta here."

They stole in along the side of the house, thorny bushes tugging at their clothes. But it was dark enough. Darryl tripped and Rhan had to thump him to keep quiet.

At the tree he stopped. Light from the window was above him, just a little farther down the wall. Close enough.

"Give me a boost up," Rhan whispered. "I'll grab the trunk. But don't go anywhere."

Darryl sighed under his breath, but he cupped his hands to make a foothold. Rhan stepped in and Darryl heaved him up fast — too fast. Rhan threw his arm around a branch, narrowly avoiding lift-off. Darryl, he realized, was a strong guy.

And it was a good thing. The trunk was too thick to get a leg around and the branch was too slender to support him. For a brief, horrible minute he thought it was going to break, but he managed to get footing on Darryl's shoulders. Rhan clung to the branch, twigs tugging his long hair, Darryl muttering and shifting under him, and then...he was inside.

It was strange to see the room from this angle; like watching TV. Everything was so clear and close. He could have counted the teacups in the china cabinet.

Lei and Garry were both leaning over a small table, working on the puzzle Rhan had glimpsed the night before. He tried to read their lips but could only follow their faces, their expressions. At one point Garry said something, and Lei threw her head back and laughed.

Rhan felt a slow tingle crawling up his neck. He remembered Garry's easy manner from the night before. He had the type of smile that could fool you, Rhan thought, if you didn't know better.

Then Lei stood up and left the room. Garry turned suddenly toward the fireplace. Rhan saw that Thalie had been sitting in a chair the whole time, holding a book but watching them.

Her face was easy to read, dark and angry, but something more. He didn't know what. When Garry spoke, she threw her book at him.

Good, good for you! Rhan cheered inside. But the man caught it skilfully, gracefully, and then sauntered over to her.

Garry laid the book on the arm of the chair. For a moment he only stood next to her, over her. Then he put his hand on her hair.

Rhan had stopped breathing. He clung to his branch, frozen, his insides twisting like someone wringing out a rag.

"My shoulders," Darryl hissed underneath him. "They're breaking!"

Thalie stood up suddenly and said something, too faint for Rhan to hear. Then she left the room. Garry looked up at the ceiling, hesitating. And then he followed her out.

The metallic grinding of the garage door shocked Rhan back to life. One car door slammed, then another.

He leapt from Darryl's shoulders to the ground, knees bursting on impact, but he barely stumbled.

He forced himself to hold still as he peered around the corner of the house watching the silver car back out of the driveway and into the road. The darkness and the angle made it impossible to guess who was inside. Garry and Lei? Or the other combination? He'd have to be closer to see. When the car reached the corner, he was released.

How fast are you, RanVan? Are you fast enough?

He sprinted after it, running across lawns so he wouldn't get caught in their rear-view mirror. It was lucky that he knew this neighbourhood a little, lucky that there were stop signs at almost every corner. He ran, eyes fastened on the car that glowed like armour under the moon. It seemed like the only light — that and his own brilliant blue streak.

The time has come, Dark Lord. The day of reckoning. Justice is on your heels and he is gaining ground...

But he wasn't. After five blocks the knight's legs

were giving out and he couldn't catch his breath. Helplessly he watched the silver car pull farther and farther ahead, then turn onto a main drag. In seconds it was out of sight.

Rhan staggered up to the last stop sign and hooked his arm around it. He leaned against it, cold metal on his burning neck. He was shaking.

You dimwit. You piece of garbage. You useless whack.

It didn't matter that he'd been racing against a machine, or that he didn't know what he'd have done if he'd caught it. He had failed.

True knights whipped each other for penance, cut themselves with knives to mark their humiliation. Rhan pulled Gran's last two cigarettes out of his pocket. One was broken and the other bent but they looked like love itself anyway. He threw them into a puddle.

Never forget how you failed today.

A few more deep breaths and he pushed himself off the pole. As he turned back toward home, he saw Darryl come around the corner at full tilt, his kinky hair wild, his face pulled white and flat like one of his own drawings. But the big boy slowed when he saw Rhan, watching him until they fell into step.

"You're starting to scare me," Darryl said quietly.

Rhan kept walking, his hands in his pockets, his heart still in his throat. He was starting to scare himself.

NINE

"I HAVE to get into that house," Rhan said. "That's all there is to it. Chasing after cars is futile, spying is futile..."

"Not to mention illegal," Darryl said sullenly.

"To beat the enemy, you have know the enemy," Rhan continued. "I've got to sit down with him, figure out how he thinks. I have to get into that house."

"Great. You going in through the window or the chimney?"

"Boys." They both jumped, startled by the sudden appearance of Mrs. Beattie, their class instructor. "This is my last warning. If you insist on visiting, you'll be doing it in the hall."

It was Monday, second period, and they were in the library researching a psychology assignment. Or that's what they were supposed to be doing. Rhan hadn't been able to bring himself to crack a book. His other assignment was burning the skin off his bones.

What he couldn't understand was Darryl's attitude. What was the matter with him? He was there on Saturday night, too, Rhan thought. He knows everything I know, almost.

He'd told Darryl what he'd seen through the window. He'd told him about Garry touching Thalie's hair.

Darryl had looked at him. "That's not assault, Rhan, no matter what you think it looks like. You can't have somebody arrested for it. It'd never hold up in a court of law."

Court of law. Rhan had no faith in the legal system, and Darryl was one of the few people who knew it. He was hurt that it should even come up.

Now Rhan leaned dejectedly on his elbow. God, he wanted a cigarette.

He hadn't noticed Darryl sketching, and was suddenly surprised as a sheet of looseleaf slid in front of him. Their old buddy, Arachnaman. But he seemed to Rhan to be more thoughtful in this version, as thoughtful as you can look with dripping fangs.

Rhan grabbed a pencil and began to write.

The time has come, Arachnaman proclaimed. *I must gather my forces for the final battle, tally my strengths. I have no money. I'm not big, or especially strong. Weapons? None to speak of. I have taken on this duel with only my wits.*

He slid the paper back to Darryl, who studied it for a long moment. He looked puzzled. When the drawing came back, Darryl had made a big arrow pointing toward Arachnaman's fangs.

How tragic that Fly Specks has developed an antidote for my poison, yet how profound! Is this not how all the great battles evolve? All powers must one day meet an anti-power, to even the balance of strength. As Supe used to say: into every life a little Kryptonite must fall.

Darryl was mystified, and getting mad. He didn't know how to draw this. He shot a hard glance at Rhan, then quickly sketched Fly Specks above their hero. An air attack was imminent.

Rhan felt his own chest tighten but near the bottom of the page he scribbled: *I will not fight you,*

Fly Specks, not until I know the reason why you seek to destroy me, and I you! Why is this? Why are we locked in this doomed quarrel —

Rhan broke off, looking at what he had written. Darryl seized the sheet and stared at it. Suddenly he folded the drawing, a straight, sharp line between Arachnaman and his opponent. He tore Fly Specks away from the hero, crumpled him up and dropped him on the table.

"There, he's dead," Darryl snapped.

"What? He can't be. Racky never laid a finger on him!"

"He had a heart attack."

"Bad guys never have heart attacks," Rhan shot back. "And this was just getting good."

"This was just getting *stupid*."

It was as if the morning had rolled up and smacked him in the face. Rhan struggled to keep his voice even.

"Darryl, the history, the background. We have to know this. Arachnaman can't keep fighting without a reason. This is important stuff."

"No, it's not," Darryl said bluntly. Then his voice lowered, almost to a plea. "He's just a spider, Rhan. I made him up."

"Once he's a superhero, he's got to follow the rules."

"No, he doesn't. He's my guy. I drew him."

Flare of fury. "He's mine, too."

"I drew him!"

"But you don't believe in him!"

They looked at each other, astonished, again, that they'd been yelling.

In the corner of his eye Rhan saw Mrs. Beattie moving in, but before she reached them, the bell ended the period. The two of them almost jammed shoulders in the library exit. Once in the hall, there was an awkward silence.

"See you," Darryl said finally. Rhan said nothing. Something was stretching inside him, opening up like a balloon.

He was determined not to go to the cafeteria. You don't have any classes down that way, he told himself stubbornly. And you're not hungry. But by the end of the third period, just before lunch, he found himself in the wrong hallway.

Well, maybe just a quick glance.

He hurried past and looked. Every table was upright and neat again, his hard work erased. He'd known it would be like this, but he still felt a small shot of disappointment.

She was right, he thought. Only the people who turned them back knew. Them and us.

But on his second pass by, he saw she was right about the other thing, too. The damaged doors were off, leaning against a wall, cardboard taped to one side to support the jagged shards. Kids on their way in for lunch stopped to stare, and whisper.

Rhan slowed, then fell in with them, his chest growing tight. The shock was fresh in daylight. Bits of glass clung to the frame like broken teeth. It was only a door but it looked *hurt*. He was thinking about Darryl and the library, about Racky and the rules. That bad guys didn't have heart failure and good guys didn't attack without a reason. He began to back away.

"A tragedy, Mr. Van."

The voice made him jump. He jerked around to see Sahota standing behind him, hands clasped behind his back.

"Mindless destruction is the gravest tragedy," Sahota continued, "don't you think?"

He knew what he thought. But what was he supposed to think?

"Well, at least nobody was injured," Rhan said. Immediately he winced. Idiot! How would you know if you weren't there! You've got to be more careful, he warned himself.

But the vice-principal didn't seem to notice, or he let it pass. "A victimless crime — is that no crime at all?"

"If a tree falls in the forest and nobody hears it, does it make a sound?" Rhan said.

Sahota looked at him, face as smooth as a copper pot. But his brown eyes were intent. "When the tree is on the ground, the sound is superfluous. Six hundred dollars to repair the doors, Mr. Van, whether they made a sound or not."

"Insurance," Rhan challenged.

"The *deductible* is six hundred dollars, money that could have gone to other things. Additional tables, perhaps?"

Was that sarcasm in his voice, or an accusation? Rhan straightened, mad and scared at the same time.

"Then you should have bought the tables before somebody smashed in your door," he snapped. He moved to leave, but Sahota stepped in front of him.

"I am farsighted, Mr. Van, but not quite clair-voyant. At least not concerning doors. Do come see me." Pause. "Should you ever have something on your mind."

The slightest shade of a bow, just enough to give the conversation a definite end. Rhan watched him go, his heart running.

By 3:30 he had given up on himself entirely. Okay, so he was weak. He had no willpower and he would have made a rotten knight. But nobody had heard him make the vow Saturday night, so it wasn't really legal, right?

Enough's enough, Rhan thought. He was going to dump his books, ignore his homework and walk straight over to Fil's for three American king-size. Mainline stuff. It would probably knock him over. Okay. He was ready to get knocked over.

Leaning into his locker, he felt a hand on his back. He tried to turn but she swept in next to him, tugging him into a huddle.

"Hi," Thalie said. Her eyes were bright with excitement, but in one glance he saw there was more. Lipgloss and perfume, even her close-cropped hair had a shine. No fantasy creature now, she was utterly female, and close.

Rhan grinned. "Hi," he said.

"How are you? How was your weekend?"

Rhan felt a twist inside. Small talk, maybe, but what if she knew? What if she'd seen him Saturday night? He hadn't even thought of it before now.

"It was fine," he said carefully.

There was a beat of silence, then she couldn't

stand it anymore. "Did you see it? Did you go in?"

The doors. Rhan was relieved. "Yeah, I was there."

"The whole school's talking about it," Thalie continued. "We couldn't have picked a better target. Rumours are running like crazy. A lot of people think it's gang work —"

"Sahota thinks it was me," Rhan blurted.

"Does he have any proof?"

"How could he have *proof*? I didn't do it!"

"Shh!" She pulled him in closer, and left her hand on his shoulder. "You have to expect a certain amount of risk," she whispered. "All the important things, the Resistance, the Underground, nobody got any guarantees. They did what was right. They didn't do what was safe."

She was near enough to make him dizzy. He blinked to clear his head.

"But they weren't stupid," Rhan insisted. "I should have thought this out better. The cafeteria — it was too close to home, if you know what I mean."

"I agree. We have to branch out into the community. This school is only a micro-organism, a symptom of a greater disease." She squeezed his shoulder. "We need to go out again."

His stomach flipped. From her voice, he knew she had something in mind, something like the cafeteria disaster. It pressed on the vow he'd made to himself. *No more broken doors, RanVan.*

But her hand gripping his shoulder seemed urgent, reminding him of his first priority.

"Okay," Rhan said finally, "I'll go. On one condition. I want to have supper at your place."

Her hand dropped and she stepped back. "Oh, God. Why?"

Because I need to sit down with the Dark Lord.

"Well, I want to meet your family, you know, for real. And I'm sure they want to meet me. I'm a great guy," he said, grinning.

No reaction. He had to push harder.

"Look," he said, lowering his voice, "I like you. I don't understand everything we do together, but at least I'm open. At least I *try*." He shrugged. "I'll be nice. I'll eat with utensils. Promise."

"You'll hate them. You'll be miserable."

"Are you...miserable?"

Thalie looked at him sharply. "Just what did Garry say to you, the day you followed me home?"

Rhan felt a flush of heat. He still felt guilty about that. And he couldn't bring himself to repeat Garry's words; it'd be like they'd been talking about her behind her back. Thalie didn't need to know she was a thing, even of beauty.

"Nothing...nothing, really," he stammered. "He talked about the pictures, photography. It's his hobby."

"His hobby," Thalie said coldly. "God, it makes him sound so *folksy*. And he'd like you to believe that, too." Her gaze wandered to the floor for a moment, then she looked back up at him, determined. "You really want to meet them? Fine. But remember, you asked for this."

"When?" Rhan said.

"What about Friday?" Thalie said. "And we'll go out together after?" Her voice seemed to hold a challenge, and he met it.

"Okay."

"But don't say I didn't warn you."

"I won't."

She leaned in suddenly, as if she might kiss him, but stopped.

"See you," she said.

Rhan walked home alone. Autumn had rolled in, pie-dough clouds that absorbed the noise of the streets. Or maybe it was a lull in traffic, the last pause before true rush hour began. The day was holding its breath.

You got so close, Rhan told himself. You were right at the edge, but not over.

He could have asked Thalie if Garry was abusing her, could have dug for the facts that would stand up in the court of law Darryl harped about. But this wasn't about the law! This was about someone's feelings, and there were places you didn't go unless you were asked. She hadn't pressed him about his parents, and he wouldn't press about this. It was only cruelty to force out the truth if you already knew it.

Why couldn't Darryl understand that! Darryl knew more about his history than anyone. Beyond that, they read the same stuff, they did the same things. But now when genuine injustice was calling them, shouting at them, Darryl could only drag his feet and argue. Rhan was more hurt than mad. How could the person who was most like you suddenly stop understanding?

He reached the Rite Shop with the first drops of rain. At the counter, Fil looked up.

"Home at last," he said. "Where you been last

coupla days, kid?"

He reached under the counter and Rhan felt the sharp bite of desire. How it would look and smell and taste.

With all his strength, he lifted his hand.

"Nah, it's okay."

Fil shrugged goodnaturedly. Rhan pulled himself away and over to Stormers, then settled down in front of the screen. When the scores came up, he saw that RanVan had fallen behind the others, miles behind, worlds behind. But it didn't matter. He wasn't playing for points anymore.

Hi, buddy.

He fell into the first level easily, like hanging up his coat and kicking off his shoes. But as he progressed, watched his little streak of blue cut down the snipers and claim the bridge to the second level, he felt a welling of understanding.

The nature of the breed, Rhan thought. That's all it was. A little bit noble, a little bit stupid. And mostly alone. That's just the way we are.

TEN

"**H**OLD it right there," Gran said, getting up from her chair.

"Hold what?" Rhan was already reaching for his jacket. "And how long do you want me to hold it?"

She caught him by the shoulders and swivelled him around to face the hallway mirror. He grinned at his reflection.

"Yeah, I know. Great-looking guy."

"In yesterday's T-shirt and grubby jeans. That's not a kid I'd like to have to supper."

"That's the kid you *always* have to supper!"

She tugged the jacket out of his hands. "Well, I still wouldn't let him out in public. Come on, you. Let's try again."

Rhan groaned, but she had his jacket. He followed her into his bedroom.

She was rifling his closet, where he kept his go-naked-first clothes.

"This is nice," Gran said, pulling out a turtleneck. Rhan retched and dropped onto the bed.

"Well, what about this shirt? She'd fall all over you."

"In a fit of laughter!"

But it was getting late, and he knew it. When Gran reached the white cotton shirt with powder-blue stripes, he held out his hand. "Okay, I give up. That'll do. I gotta go."

She passed it to him and he thought she left. But when he'd pulled off his T-shirt he saw that she was leaning against the door frame, watching him. A faint smile had settled at the corners of her mouth.

He slipped on the new shirt hurriedly. "What are you grinning at?" he said.

"Oh, I don't know. Just thinking." There was a pause. "Is she nice, this girl?"

Rhan hesitated. He'd been thinking about Thalie a lot this past week, but nice was too pale a word, somehow.

"I guess. I mean, yeah, of course."

"She must be pretty special, if you're meeting her parents," Gran said. He didn't answer. It was new to him, this tone of voice. Curious but careful, as if she didn't want to intrude. As if, Rhan thought in wonder, there were two adults in the room.

He finished the buttons and looked up. She was still there, still smiling. "*What*?" he said again.

Gran shrugged, light and girlish. "Well, in *my* day, when a fella was invited to have dinner with a girl's parents..."

"He just flagged down a dinosaur and sped right over!"

"Oh, you!" She threw his jacket at him and left. He pulled it on and checked the mirror quickly, but when he tried to get out of his room, her voice rang through the suite.

"Pants, too!"

Rhan sighed. So much for adulthood.

When he finally made it to the front door, he did a turn for inspection.

"There. Happy now?"

"Perfect," Gran said, beaming. "I'd date you

myself."

The night welcomed him like an old friend. Barely seven o'clock, it was already dark. You could smell the change in the air, even if you couldn't see it yet, Rhan thought. He loved October, or he loved this one. It still rained but a steady breeze pushed the clouds off fast. The moon and sometimes stars lit up the wet streets, and if you stood in the right place, you could even see the mountains.

Rhan felt he was standing in the right place. In a few weeks he would be sixteen, on Halloween. He hadn't gone trick-or-treating in years, but it was still a great day to have a birthday. He'd always felt the whole world was having a party just for him.

Well, it's not your party tonight, he reminded himself. He only had a few hours to study Garry at close range. Somehow before he left the house he had to know this man, what his strengths were, and his weaknesses. There was a chink in everyone's armour, if you could only find it.

It bothered him a little that he still didn't know what he wanted to accomplish, what the ultimate end of all this would be. Make Garry move out? But it was his house. Force Garry to stop by threatening him with exposure? But he couldn't act on that bluff; he wouldn't risk shaming Thalie, too. Maybe he should take his cues from her, let her decide the course of action. After all, she was the one he was fighting for.

Rhan's heart skipped, a leap of nerves and excitement. But he wasn't afraid. The whole night stretched out in front of him and he was revved, ready for it. It was almost Halloween. And the moon was so close he could have reached up and grabbed it out of the sky.

•

He hadn't realized how tall Lei was. Standing in the doorway wasn't the same as standing next to her. But that had been a different day, too. Today he was a guest and she seemed to hover like a willowy phantom. Could she take his coat? Would he like something to drink? Why didn't he relax in the front room?

But Rhan couldn't relax. He wasn't often a guest, and he was shocked to discover it was work. For once he only wanted to sit and watch, but he couldn't get out of the spotlight.

Thalie wasn't much help. While Lei swooped in and out of the room, she sat draped in a chair near the cold fireplace, another phantom, dark and remote. She seemed determined not to talk to him. When Rhan tried, her responses were low and indifferent. He was frustrated. How was he supposed to get his cues?

He stole glances rather than meet her eyes. She was wearing black on black. It made her face look pale and eerie. Black-lined eyes and painted lips, a bright streak on each cheek. It was, he realized, the face of the girl who had tumbled from the car in front of the Rite Shop.

"Well, hiya, dude. We meet again."

Garry was in the doorway, hands in his pockets. Rhan stood up, alert.

"Yeah, I guess we do," he said, as cordially as he

could. Then, nothing. Thalie's silence was almost palpable. Oh, God, where was Lei? Anyone!

"You finished the puzzle?" Rhan asked finally, desperately. It wasn't on the coffee table.

"That one? Oh, yeah. We're into this one now."

Garry walked across the room and hit a wall switch. There was a small dining-room table Rhan hadn't noticed before, and stretched across it was the beginning of a large puzzle. It drew him over, almost against his will. Most of the border was done, and patches here and there, all of them black and white. It seemed to him to be some kind of checkerboard, until he glimpsed the box lid on a chair.

Rhan stared. He had never seen anything like this before. It was a superb line drawing of night turning into day, of fish turning into birds. At the outside edges, the images were opposites, subtly shifting until the middle, where they were both, or neither. It was a crisp, precise rendering of the impossible.

Transformation. Rhan looked up, not sure if he'd said the word out loud.

"Wild, huh?" Garry was grinning. "It's from a picture by a guy named Escher. I love his stuff."

"Wild," Rhan agreed.

"But deadly."

"What?"

"You get hooked on these things," Garry said. He ran his hand over a finished section. "You just get started on the border and the next thing you know it's two o'clock in the morning. And you can't stay away. Every time you go past, you gotta stop and find another piece." He shrugged. "Get a little fix, you know?"

Rhan didn't know. He'd started one puzzle in his life, and had thrown it out half-finished. But he knew other things he couldn't stay away from. Whole nights of one level and one level and one level more.

"These big ones aren't easy," Garry continued. "It's a different technique. You can't follow the picture — it's too confusing. You've got to look at the pieces, the colour and the shape of them. I'm pretty good once I get into it. But Thalie's the best, aren't you, Thal?"

Rhan looked. He'd almost forgotten about her. But her painted, stony eyes were still focused on some secret distance.

"It's pretty cold in here," Garry said, and he winked. "Maybe I should start a fire."

But just then Lei called them all for supper.

They ate in yet another room. How many did this place have? Rhan wondered. The house was even bigger than he'd first imagined. Lei sat at the head of the table across from Thalie. Rhan was facing Garry.

"Boy, girl, boy, girl," Thalie remarked. "How quaint."

He looked at her, but no one else responded.

"Do you like seafood, Rhan?" Lei asked, passing him the serving dish.

"Love it," he answered cheerfully. *It makes me sick.*

"Well, this dish is originally Japanese, but it's spread throughout the Asian countries, and finally into North America. I'll bet you've never heard of it."

"You're probably right." *Please, I don't want to know.*

"It's called sashimi," Lei continued excitedly. "Something of a variation of sushi, but the seaweed and green mustard make all the difference. I'm sure you can't even tell that it's raw."

"I'd never have known." *Oh, my God.*

"I actually saw it on a bistro menu last week and I'm delighted to see Canadians embracing more natural food. It's — "

"High priced *and* low cal," Thalie interrupted sharply. "Perfect for someone who's fanatical about her weight and her status."

Lei's fork hovered. She glared across the table, but she wasn't beat.

"Well, I think it's important to care about what image you present. That's how the world judges you, whether you like it or not. You wouldn't, for example, walk into a hair salon and say, 'Give me the ugliest haircut in the city.'"

"It's my head!"

"What a pity you don't use it."

The whole meal was like that. Rhan's stomach was in knots. When he and Gran fought they just blew up at each other and that was it. He didn't understand this, conversation like sniper shots, or cold silences that hung on for minutes at a time. He'd come tonight to watch, to plan, but it was all he could do to stay out of the line of fire.

And Garry. He was right across the table, but it was easy to lose sight of him with everything else going on. Unruffled, congenial, he seemed to be eating in a completely different house.

A sane house, Rhan thought in despair. But he was determined to draw something out of the man.

"So, how's the market for new software?" he asked abruptly.

Garry looked puzzled. "I really don't know. It's not my thing."

The lie ran through him like a needle. Rhan looked at Thalie, but she wouldn't meet his eyes.

"What...what is your thing? What do you do?" he said.

Garry smiled through a mouthful, then swallowed. "I'm a developer. Construction. Maybe you've seen some of our projects — Hargrave, Belmont?"

"New divisions?"

"No, old houses, perfectly good old homes, bulldozed for greed," Thalie blurted. "Destroyed to build enormous, bloated monsters for an obscene profit!"

"I fill a need." Garry shrugged. "So does every other business. Besides, I'm not the only developer who recycles ramshackle old buildings in the city."

"But do they get their friends at the bank to phone them the *day* of foreclosure, so they can swoop in like some vulture — "

"Enough!" Lei stood up, her face stiff with fury. "I'm sorry, Rhan, but I can't take this anymore. I can't take this spoiled brat who has no respect for what puts a roof over her head."

Thalie stood, too. "And what puts a roof over

your head? Your *art?*"

Rhan held his breath. Oh, God, what was this turning into? But Garry suddenly leaned across the table toward him.

"Hey, dude. I just got a new toy. Why don't we go out to the garage and have a look?"

Only a door separated the garage from the house, but Rhan closed it behind him with relief. He just needed a breather, a chance to sort things through. His head was spinning.

How could a night have gone so totally, completely off track? And why had she lied to him?

Garry was over at a shelf on the wall. From out of the clutter he pulled a package of cigarettes.

"My own house," he said mischievously, "and I have to smoke in the garage. Oh, well. It causes less hassle. They think I quit."

He held one out to Rhan.

No, thanks.

But his hand took it, snapped it up with embarrassing speed. And the rest of the moves, finding his matches, the grind of the striker, the sudden flare, all like steps in a dance he couldn't forget. He was flooded with gratitude, and shame. So he blew it. Well, he was the only one who knew.

Garry was grinning at him. "I thought so," he said.

"What?"

"It's my talent. I have a sixth sense for people in need."

His tone made Rhan uneasy — too intimate, somehow. A conspirator. "So where's this toy?" he said gruffly.

Garry walked around his silver car to a tarp-covered mound on the other side of the garage. It reminded Rhan of Lei's sculptures, but only for an instant. Garry grabbed the tarp with his free hand and swept it off with a flourish.

"Here she is, my baby," he said proudly.

Rhan stared. This wasn't a motorcycle, it was a mirage. An old Harley-Davidson, maybe twenty years old, but in superb condition, *mint* condition, he realized, studying the black metal and brilliant chrome.

But he couldn't concentrate. Voices were filtering through the wall, the rise and fall of anger. He felt a tug of alarm.

"A friend and I rebuilt her piece by piece, with original parts," Garry said, trailing his hand along the seat. "Some I even had to hunt down in California."

"*...and you never...*"

"*Why couldn't you...*"

"But it was worth it," Garry said. "Isn't she beautiful?"

"*...lying bitch!*"

Am I the only one who isn't deaf? Rhan wondered. Couldn't he hear it, too? It no longer seemed natural, Garry's calm.

"I'd be out on her every day, but you know women." Garry rolled his eyes. "They get mad about the littlest things."

"I think one of them's already mad at you," Rhan said.

"Thalie? Oh, she gets into these moods, but it's not serious. You just have to know how to handle her."

"Like pushing her out of a car?" Rhan said. "Is that the way?"

Garry straightened. For a second the congenial face was split, broken open in astonishment. Then he caught himself, and the shiny surface returned. It was, Rhan realized, something he worked very hard at.

"Is that what she told you?" he said.

"That's what I saw."

Garry seemed to look the slightest bit relieved — for someone who wasn't worried.

"Then you just learned something. Your eyes lied to you. She jumped, man." Garry shrugged easily. "The lady wanted out and she got out."

Rhan's heart was pounding.

"I don't believe you."

"So don't, but don't take everything she says as gospel, either. She's a chick with a pretty wild imagination. Cool-headed guy like you is just what she needs." His voice lowered, the way it had in the photograph room that first time. "Hang in there. She'll be worth your while, if you know what I mean."

Rhan's stomach swept up in revulsion, and he spun around toward the door. If he didn't go, he'd kill him or get sick or something. But when he touched the doorknob, Garry spoke.

"Just one word of advice, dude. Look at the pieces, not the picture."

Rhan almost bowled over Thalie in the hallway. Tears had destroyed her make-up; black bled into pink.

"Do you want to come out with me now?" he

97

said. She nodded, and in moments, it seemed, they were outside, holding hands, walking fast.

The night was gathering inside him, a windstorm into a bay. He could barely believe how Garry had encouraged him, almost offered Thalie to him as if she were a lamp, or a picture on the wall. As if she was his to give, Rhan thought. The man seemed like the breath of evil itself.

And yet, something Garry had said struck a nerve. Something about Thalie's imagination.

"Why did you lie to me?" Rhan said suddenly.

Thalie's hand stiffened in his. "About what?"

"About Garry. How he makes a living."

There was a pause as she wiped her face with her sleeve. "It embarrasses me," she said, "feeling like I do. After the things I said, well, I thought you would think I was two-faced, a traitor," she finished bitterly.

"Didn't you trust me?"

"Not then. I...I'm careful about what I tell people."

But her hand in his seemed to say she trusted him now, a bit.

"Why did you cut your hair?"

She drew a breath, the beginning of a sigh.

"Weren't you there tonight? Didn't you see? Nobody takes me seriously. I can talk and talk and it's like they're looking through me, like I'm not really there."

With a chill, Rhan saw Garry in the garage again, stroking the bike.

"I just wanted them to look at me, force them to look at me, even if I had to be ugly to do it..."

"I don't think you're ugly." And he didn't. Car

headlights lit her up as they passed, the smeared face and wrought-iron eyes. She was more captivating than she had ever been. He could barely take his eyes away.

There was one more question he could have asked, about how she'd really left the silver car on the first night they'd met. But it didn't seem to matter anymore. He'd had dinner with the Dark Lord and he'd heard enough. It was time to do something.

"I think you were right," he said. "I think we have to branch out, raise social consciousness in the community..."

She squeezed his hand. She was with him, ahead of him.

"And I think we should start on Belmont," Thalie said.

ELEVEN

IRST level: speed and agility. Save time, save the power for when you need it.

Go like hell, RanVan.

Back lane to back lane, cutting across lawns and the park. Thalie knew the way but he was leading; labyrinths were a personal challenge to him. It was barely ten o'clock but he was moving fast, momentum pushing him on.

He had begun the advance, the first bold strike, not on the castle — not yet — but on its outpost. In his mind's eye he could see himself, a blur of light moving through night country, and the distant stone tower that was His stronghold.

Build your puzzles, Dark Lord, build your kingdoms, but you cannot stay my hand. There is no fortress that is impenetrable, no wall that won't come down...

"There," Thalie said suddenly. "That's it."

They had come up on it from behind, through the unlit alley, and the structure seemed to loom out of nowhere. Rhan slowed, then stopped. Garry was building a monster, all right. Sprawled over two lots, the framework nudged its neighbours' fences; he couldn't see how far it went out in front. Bare beams soared up like dinosaur bones.

Rhan didn't know much about construction but he could see the thing coming together. The main floor was framed and the outer walls were up. At one end work had just begun on the ceiling, which would be the floor to the second storey.

"Okay, now what?" Thalie whispered.

He didn't answer because he didn't know.

It wasn't supposed to be so big, Rhan thought, drifting cautiously toward the lot. It wasn't supposed to be so *solid*. And what about all the neighbours, and passing traffic? What about passing police traffic?

Second level: strength of purpose.

The flutterkick of shame made him wince. *If he can beat you now, without even being here, you're dead meat, RanVan.*

The next thing he knew he was swinging through the big opening that was scheduled to be the back door. Thalie followed him inside, trailing at a distance. He was acutely aware of her eyes on his back, and he strode purposefully from one room to the next, trying to come up with a plan.

But he had no brainstorms. Minutes passed and Thalie drifted off on her own. Rhan could feel the sweat gathering in the crevices under his clothes. *You should have brought something, idiot! A crowbar, a bulldozer, something! This isn't a freaking kit. What kind of damage did you think you could do with your bare —*

His leg hit wood and he stumbled, swearing in pain.

"What happened?" Thalie called from another room.

Rhan limped around to see what had tripped him. He could just make out the long two-by-four leaning at an angle from the floor to the top of the wall. *Bloody stupid place to leave a board.* In spite he kicked at it with the leg that didn't hurt. The wall shuddered but the board held. Rhan stared in amazement. It had been nailed in place.

"Are you okay?" Thalie was getting mad now, but he barely noticed. His mind was on fire.

A brace, that's what it was. And there were more of them all down the side of the house. Because the ceiling wasn't on yet, the outer shell was held up only by the dividing walls.

And these braces.

He whammed the two-by-four again. Nails screamed as they tore from the wood, then the board clattered to the floor. He hurried to the next brace, his heart pounding.

"For God's sake, what are you doing!" Thalie dashed over. Rhan whipped around.

"Stay back! The wall could go!"

She froze. He could feel her looking at him, taking it all in. For a second he held his breath — they hadn't talked about what they'd do when they got here.

But when she spoke, she sounded delighted. "We'll just have to keep the noise down or somebody will call the cops."

Now it became work. Rhan kicked carefully at the braces to loosen the nails, then tugged the boards out with his hands. The raw wood scraped ridges into his palms, and sweat ran in a stream down his back.

But the sound of it, the sweet sensation of the boards as they were wrenched apart. He had never felt so strong.

No more broken doors.

The words came out of nowhere, like a whisper behind his back. He hesitated, then heaved with renewed fury.

That was different. We weren't dealing with a monster then. We weren't dealing with true injustice! The reason, Rhan thought grimly, changes all the rules.

After the sixth brace he stepped away, trying not to gasp. There were more of them — maybe another four — but he thought he could see the long wall starting to bow. What if it went before he was ready? What if it fell the wrong way? For the first time it occurred to him he might be in danger.

"Okay," he called to Thalie softly, "get out of here and start running. I'll catch up."

"No. I want to see this."

"Look, I don't know what's going to happen — "

"I don't care! We're in this together. It's mine, too." He had come to know that determined sound in her voice. And it was exciting to have an audience.

"All right, but go outside and watch through the door," he said. He pushed on the wall, an experimental nudge, and leapt back. It seemed to wobble, but it held.

"Harder," Thalie called.

Rhan gritted his teeth and charged with his shoulder. The impact jarred him, sent him staggering. When he looked up, he was in a dream. In slow motion, the wall seemed to swell and ripple, and then it fell back, groaning in pain, tearing away from the bearing walls. The braces he'd left didn't even slow the thundering wave as it crashed down onto the neighbour's fence.

Rhan stared. His heart was on the roof of his mouth, like the first crest of a rollercoaster before the plunge, before the screams. From far away someone was calling him, but he couldn't move, couldn't stop staring. It was extraordinary. Extraordinarily unreal.

"What in hell is going on!"

Rhan looked. Through the woodwork, on the front lawn, he could just see a white streak, the size of an undershirt. A big undershirt. That was real enough. Realization booted him through the back door — almost in one leap — and then he was sprinting down the dark lane, where Thalie had been waiting.

The labyrinth again, trying to remember all the twists and turns. Part of him was running scared. Had they been seen? Were they being followed? The other part of him was still riding it, the groaning crash, the rush of dust, the reverberations through the floorboards. He could go so fast, riding that wave. Tonight he could have caught the silver car, he could have lifted it over his head.

They ran as far as the park, to the yellow tubes, and crawled inside. Just to rest, Rhan told himself. Just to think.

But he didn't do either.

"We did it," Thalie whispered, pulling off his glasses. "We did it." Kissing his face, his mouth, his neck. He was so surprised he could barely keep up, but he tried. He tried.

That shock was overtaken by another. Bare skin. She had tugged his shirt up high around his ribs, then her own. Now she slid in against him, and a searing rush of heat pulled his voice out of his throat.

Rhan's feet were wet. He'd been standing in the damp grass for so long, knocking on Darryl's window. But he couldn't believe Darryl was asleep — it didn't feel that late — or that he'd forgotten their old code: three knocks, then two.

When he thought about it, the code was kind of dumb. Darryl didn't get enough people at his bedroom window to screen calls. But it was something they'd always done, so he did it now. Three knocks, then two, over and over.

The glass slid open abruptly, and Rhan jumped, startled. It was Darryl, all right, half asleep but in the flesh.

"What?" he asked groggily.

"Come out, I want you to see something," Rhan said.

Darryl blinked and twisted around, probably to look at his clock radio. Then he whipped back.

"It's almost midnight!"

Rhan was surprised. "Oh, yeah?"

"Yeah!"

"But it's Friday night," Rhan coaxed, grinning. "Live it up. This won't take long."

Darryl eyed him stonily. Briefly Rhan wondered if he was mad about something. Had they argued? He couldn't remember, and he shrugged the thought away.

"Come on, Darryl. This is important."

Darryl sighed tiredly. "I get caught again and I'm up the creek, Rhan. No shit! I just can't, I..."

"Is she going to run your life forever?"

It was a low blow, and he knew it. It was a rotten, mean thing to say to a friend. But it worked.

"Oh, Jesus." Darryl pulled himself away from the window, muttering. "Jesus H. Christ..."

In less than a minute he was dressed and squeezing through the window. He dropped to the ground with an ungainly thud.

"This better be good..." he grumbled, staggering up. But Rhan was already at the far edge of the yard.

He led Darryl through the streets with barely a word. He hadn't expected it to be so late, or his friend to be so grouchy. Every once in a while he felt an anxious pull, wondering if it was the right thing, bringing in a witness. And then it would whip through him again: fire and lightning and Christmas Day.

He needs this, Rhan thought. He needs to *see*.

Walking Thalie home, he'd thought this out carefully. It wasn't that Darryl didn't believe. He just needed a higher level of proof. If Darryl could see the wall — the one he'd brought down with his bare hands — he'd have to believe in how real this was.

At the top of the block, Rhan stopped. The residential street was deep with quiet. If the police had been here, they were gone now, but maybe still prowling about.

"Okay," Rhan said softly. "Just pretend we're walking down the street."

"We *are* just walking down the street." But Darryl followed anyway.

Across the road from the site, Rhan said, "There. That's it."

He didn't have to say what "it" was; the carnage was still fresh. The wall almost reached the neighbour's house, and what was left of the fence lay toppled on the grass. From this angle, the front, Rhan could see how the tearing had pulled on the framework; it listed drunkenly. A strong wind or more pressure could have collapsed the other walls like a house of cards. He could see now the danger he'd been in.

"Who did this?" Darryl's voice was barely above a whisper.

"Us," Rhan said. "Me."

Darryl looked at him for a long moment, then charged back up the sidewalk the way he'd come.

"Wait." Rhan scrambled after him. "You don't even know — "

"I know this is sick, that's what I know!"

"It's not like somebody owns the place. It belongs to *him*!" All the way up to the top of the street, he tried to explain. How he'd been at Thalie's for supper, how it had been, and inside the garage.

"The man is a monster, Darryl."

"So let her press charges, Rhan. Don't you get it? This way you're the one who's breaking the law. You're the one who's going to get caught."

Rhan hesitated. He'd never thought of it in those terms before: breaking the law. Darryl seized on the silence.

"You've got to get out of this thing, Rhan. God, she's just tangling you up. Using you. It's like you're obsessed, and it's getting worse! One day you're spying through windows and next you're pushing down walls?"

"She needs my help — "

"Then *help* her. Tell Guidance at Bedford, or go to the police. They know how to handle this stuff."

"Oh, do they?" Rhan said bitterly.

Darryl looked at him, a gaze as clear and dangerous as a broken piece of glass.

"I hate to say this..."

"Then don't."

"But you've got to hear it. Whatever you're doing for this girl, it won't bring your mom back."

"Shithead." Wave over wave of fire. "Like I'm an idiot? Like I don't know that? Shithead! You have no understanding. You don't have the beginning — " He stopped and switched tracks.

"Don't you know who I am?" Rhan said.

Darryl's eyes widened.

"There's something, Darryl. I swear it, I swear to God! It's like this energy, this power — "

"Stop it, Rhan. Don't talk crazy!"

" — like a superhero. I can feel it and it's real. I even have another name..."

"Stop it, just stop!" Darryl looked frightened, near tears. "You're losing your grip, Rhan. This isn't a comic, for Christ's sake! Stuff like that doesn't happen to real people. I wish to God that it did, but it's in your head."

For a single still moment they just looked at each other. Then Rhan stepped back. Away.

"You need to see a doctor," Darryl pleaded. "A shrink. You need help with this."

Turning around. Walking away. Fingernails digging into his palms, he was holding it so hard. But he wouldn't let go. One step and one step and one step more.

So now you know. He can imagine it, but he can't believe it.

When he finally turned the corner onto his own street, his heart skipped. His night vision wasn't great at this distance, but there was no missing the big white blur two blocks away. Not someone for the Rite Shop. Fil would have closed long ago.

The fear was a sudden, painful cramp. And then he was running, feet drumming like a prayer on the pavement. Not an ambulance, not an ambulance...

It was the Eldorado. Rhan slowed to an unsteady walk, swamped with relief. But as he drew closer, even as the fear unwound, it began to twist into something else.

Who did he think he was, this guy? Some kind of vampire, who could only do business at night? What right did he have, scaring people to death?

Gust of fury.

And he probably enjoyed it. The prick, the tyrant!

This time there was no hesitation, no practice. He swept in on the big white car, planted one hand on the hood and kicked hard. He felt the satisfying burst of metal under his foot, then the side mirror hit the ground and shattered.

Rhan stared at the pieces. It seemed to be getting shorter and shorter, the space between wanting to do something and actually doing it.

When he opened the door to the suite, Gran was sitting alone at the dinette. Eldorado was standing in the living-room.

"Hey," Rhan said. "There were some guys around your car."

Alarm on the flabby face.

"I think they did something," Rhan insisted. "But they took off when I showed up. That way." He tilted his head north.

In seconds the landlord was outside; through the screen Rhan heard him swear. The boy closed the inner wooden door slowly, watching Eldorado bolt into the car and screech away — north. If justice had a sound, that was it.

But some might be coming his way, too. He had to have a story, and a good one, for being this late.

He turned and shrugged, a little sheepishly. "Geez, I thought I was never going to get out of there."

Gran didn't answer.

"You know, they're nice people, but I don't think they get much company," Rhan continued. "They had to show me everything. Thalie's mom, well, she's this artist, this sculptor, and her stuff is neat but kind of weird..."

Gran seemed to be looking past him, through him. Rhan heard his voice quicken nervously.

"...I mean, I almost said I thought it was a couch — isn't that a riot? And...oh, yeah! Then we all started this puzzle, these people are just hooked on puzzles, and we barely got the border done and I couldn't believe what time it was — "

Gran looked up at him, and he froze.

"That's it, love," she said dully. "He sold the place. They're going to level it and put up condos.

We'll get a settlement if we're out by Halloween."
The faintest crackle, like a dry leaf. "Happy birthday."

And RanVan the Defender sat down at the
dinette and smoked three of his grandmother's
cigarettes, one after the other.

TWELVE

HE dreamed he was playing the game. He dreamed he was running down a corridor, flying over the wet stone floor that glimmered blue as he passed. That light was his only guide, and the fact that he knew the way. He had been here and been here, but this time he was going to make it.

The scrambling, scratching of feet behind him, echoing off the stone. A horrible sound, like enormous insects hurrying to overtake him. He wanted to turn and fire into them, clean them away no matter how long it took. But he knew the game. They were no real danger, only a distraction meant to waste his time. They could stall him to death.

Don't look, don't listen. Keep going.

The first bridge appeared suddenly, and he couldn't halt the gut rush of relief. But this was trickery, too; there were snipers waiting for him to try to cross. He had to hold his ground somehow, let the snipers gather on the bridge and dodge their fire, wait it out even as the insect guards closed in on his back.

The squeeze. You know this. Don't panic. You know this.

And he did. He gritted his teeth and hung on until the bridge was swarming, and then he let fly, a blazing blue shaft of justice that cut through their dark numbers like a scythe.

With the bridge swept clear he bounded onto it, jubilant that he'd done everything right, maybe for the first time. But as he touched the ground on the other side, the familiar second level disappeared.

He was in another hallway, only bigger, grander than he'd ever been in before. And quiet. No scuttling guards, no blow torches, even his own feet were soundless on the stone. Quiet and empty, except for the enormous oak door at the end of the hall.

He could barely breathe.

It can't be, I couldn't be here yet...

He didn't believe it and he didn't dare not. Maybe he'd hit a secret passage. Maybe he'd done the right thing at just the right time and triggered a warp.

He crept forward, laser ready, expecting a trick, an ambush, but inside he knew this was it. Last level. By magic or skill he was here and there was only one monster left.

He aimed the laser at the door lock, heart shaking his body, terrified but triumphant.

Just hang on, I'm here now. I'll get you out. I made it and I'll get you out.

Blue burned a hole where the metal used to be. He leapt back, braced for battle, but there was nothing. The silence was bigger than any sound.

Come on, Dark Lord. Let's do it. Come on!

Nerves stretched, tearing, he couldn't wait anymore. Gripping his weapon with two hands, he pushed on the door with his foot. It swung open without resistance into the room of a house where he used to live.

He tried to shield his eyes from the light. Heavy afternoon sun was bleeding through the venetian slats, swamping the room, drowning it. It could knock you over, that sun, it could put you to sleep. It could put two people to sleep, there in the middle of the floor...

Rhan awoke in sweat-damp sheets, his jaw aching from grinding his teeth. That it was Monday, that he was fifteen, seemed like a gift he could barely believe was for him. He rolled himself up in the blankets tight, a cocoon.

It's okay. Like saying it to someone else. It's all right.

•

"You disappoint me, Mr. Van."

Rhan kept walking without looking up. Oh, great. Oh, wonderful. Like I needed this!

He'd been on his way outside for the lunch break, just to wander around by himself. Too many people in the school today, too many people in his head.

And yet there was something about this man that challenged him, ignited what Darryl's mother would have called his smart mouth.

"If *I* can disappoint *you*, then you're basing your happiness on something outside yourself," Rhan replied, monotone. "Plan on being frustrated for the rest of your life."

Sahota hesitated; he almost stopped. "That's... that's very profound, Mr. Van."

"No, it's chapter fifteen, *Beginning Psychology*. We're not there yet but I read ahead."

This time Sahota did stop, and he laughed out loud. By the time he'd caught up, Rhan was passing an exit, but something in him wasn't quite ready to go yet. There was another door out a few hallways ahead.

"Psychology." Sahota seemed to taste the word. "Are you enjoying it?"

"It's all right," Rhan admitted, "but flaky."

"Flaky?"

"You know, cream puff stuff. The kind of course you take so you don't have to take something hard."

Sahota looked stricken. It occurred to Rhan just what kind of doctor he probably was.

"Well, don't get me wrong, it's interesting, but how many of us could make a living at it?"

"Ahh, gainful employment — a worthy goal."

"Right. And what if you went through all that work and couldn't get a job and had to do something else?"

"Such as an administrative educator in a high school? There is always that grave danger."

Rhan caught himself grinning. This guy could be funny. But sideways; you had to listen.

Another exit. Rhan let it pass. They were walking in step now, although he didn't know how. His legs were a lot shorter than the vice-principal's. One of them was adjusting stride, but he wasn't sure who.

"If not psychology, what then?" Sahota asked. "What field of endeavor do you plan to overwhelm?"

"Justice." The word was out before he could stop it.

"Law?"

"No, not exactly."

"Police sciences?"

"No." His face had begun to burn the way paper burns, from the edges in.

"I see. Then you're apt to be disappointed. The pay scale for vigilantes is very slight — although the media coverage is excellent."

Rhan was stung. "I'm not a vigilante. I just don't believe things happen the way they should."

"The way they should," Sahota repeated thoughtfully. "How easy that is to say. Condemnation requires no answers, no better plan. But to see a specific weakness and work to correct it from *within* the system — "

"I won't work for the system because the system doesn't work!"

"Aha! Generalities again." Sahota was enjoying himself. "Come, Mr. Van, you are too intelligent for that. Train yourself to deal in specifics. If you have no target then you have no hope of success."

The little blaze had become a bonfire. But he was almost at the next exit and he quickened his pace, eyes fixed on it.

Just get there, he told himself. Just get out of this.

Sahota didn't seem to notice that they were moving faster. "All change begins with a focus, a goal," he continued. "When you can target a specific wrong, however small, that is the beginning of a process. Only then can you start — "

Rhan had reached the door and he leaned on the bar, then hesitated.

"Restraining order," he said without turning. "Is that specific enough for you? As if people who need to be restrained would obey a piece of paper. Except that's all they get, until they do something. Except then it's too late."

The bar made a dull clang as he pushed against it. Then he was walking through the drizzle, through the parking lot. He thought he heard his name, his first name, squeeze out as the door eased shut behind him. It hit his shoulders and slid off to the pavement.

Gran looked up when he opened the door. It was hours before school let out, and she knew it. But she knew a lot.

"Bad day?" she said.

He nodded, grateful not to talk.

"Me, too." Gran gestured at the newspapers spread out on the coffee table in front of her. "What do you think of this one? *Wanted, experienced caretaker for 14 units. Must live on site. Couple preferred.*" Gran squinted at the ad. "Oh, hell. I didn't notice that last part. Well, we're sort of a couple, hey?"

Rhan didn't answer. Without taking off his jacket he wandered over and sat on the floor by her feet, his back against the couch.

"Oh, here's another," Gran said. "*Caretaking opportunity in seniors complex.* Well, I know you'd love that. *Mechanical and electrical experience a must...*"

He could feel her hand on the back of his head, running over his hair, tugging it gently into a pony-tail. No thinking, only touching, the way you'd pat a cat. He was too old for this. He was too old for this but just for now he couldn't bring himself to move.

"Do you ever dream about them?" he said.

Gran stopped reading. He heard her take a breath.

"No. I dream she's still a little girl and under my feet all the time. Get away. Go do something, I say, like I'm still young and we got nothing but time. That's what I dream."

The suite was quiet, quiet the way a valley would be, with the world rising up on both sides.

"Did she love him?" An old question, but some answers you had to hear and hear.

"She loved something about him, or she needed something," Gran said, "but I don't know what. 'He's crazy for me,' she'd say. And even after she left him and he scared her so bad, that's how she explained it. 'He's crazy for me.'"

Her hand on his neck, cool fingers easing free the strands that had caught under his collar.

"But you she loved. Don't you never worry about that. You were Christmas on Halloween."

Chokehold on his throat, but he had to ask. "Do you ever think...do you ever think there was something..."

"I could have done to stop it?" Gran sighed. "Oh, my boy. For nine years I've been holding that one. Go to sleep with it, wake up with it. What could I have said different? What could I have done? Nine years and all I can believe is that some love's like a loaded gun, walking around ready to blow, no matter who, no matter what. I could have run him over with a car ten years ago. I could have done that."

Trembling inside, teetering on the edge of it, closing his eyes against it.

And would you. If you had known. Would you.

THIRTEEN

RAIN, rain, and more rain. This was autumn, too. Rhan arrived at school wet, and came home the same way, and wondered if people could mildew.

He didn't look for Thalie and he avoided the places they were likely to meet. Part of him was ashamed but the other part of him knew the truth: he wasn't ready. The things they did together required energy, strength of purpose. Right now he couldn't muster enough of either. Even though he worried about her, he suspected there was some steel in her slender frame, the determination he heard so often in her voice. She could hang on just for awhile.

He didn't look for Darryl, and that was hard, too. He went days, it seemed, without hearing his own voice. It made him realize how little he talked to other kids at Bedford, and that for somebody to get mad at you, they at least had to listen to you.

He saw Darryl sometimes, staring straight ahead in their psychology class or trudging down the hallways close to the lockers. Once he saw him in the library, hunched over his open notebook, sketching furiously. He knew without looking what world Darryl was in, and the urge to walk over and dive into it was sudden and strong.

Rhan put his hand on a bookshelf and hung on. No, he told himself. He couldn't hang around somebody who didn't believe in him. These days it was hard enough believing in himself.

You live it or you don't, Rhan thought. He

pushed off the shelf and turned away, again.

He spent his evenings at the Rite Shop. Fil had moved the machines to the back of the store.

"Don't take it personal. The noise was driving me nuts," he explained.

But Rhan was relieved to be hidden away. He plunged gratefully into Stormers' world, opening every door, wandering down every corridor. He was certain that he'd missed some important clue along the way, and if he just kept at it and kept at it, he would find it. Like finding the right sequence on a combination safe.

On Thursday the weather turned: drizzle became a downpour. Rhan arrived at school soaked to the skin, his glasses streaming. He tried to dry them on his shirt and smudged them so bad he couldn't read the numbers on his locker combo. While he was fumbling with it, the final bell rang. He thumped the metal door so hard he left a dent.

At lunch he took one look at the line in the cafeteria and gave up. The rain had driven everyone inside. Kids who usually went home to eat were jostling with the crowd that didn't. Rhan stuck his hands in his pockets and started wearily toward the school store.

But that wasn't any better. The tiny room was packed. There was no line-up, just a mass of kids pushed against the counter and clustered around the vending machines. Rhan wedged himself into the crowd, frustration slowly burning a trail from his stomach to his face.

Were they blind? Couldn't they see how it was? You couldn't run a school like this! Sooner or later something had to give. Sooner or later —

"Hey, I was just going to put money in that!"

Rhan swivelled around toward the voice, with everybody else. A man in a blue work uniform was loading a vending machine onto a dolly.

"Sorry, kid, it's got to go. And the other one, too."

"They're not out of order," the boy insisted.

"No, they're not," the man said. "But the work sheet says I gotta collect 'em."

The people who'd been waiting their turn let out a collective groan that was followed by a low grumble from the rest of the room.

The news seemed to hit Rhan in the chest.

"Wait a minute," he blurted out loud. "You can't just take it. Nobody asked us."

Ripple of agreement. One definite "Yeah!"

The man pulled back on the dolly handles, tipping the machine for transport.

"Talk...to...your...principal," he gasped, and wheeled it out the door. There was a moment of silence — disbelief — that was quickly filled by the swirl of conversation. Everybody was mad, whether they'd been waiting for the machines or not.

Rhan was standing perfectly still, counting to ten.

Let it go, he told himself. You know this shit and you know what it got you. Just let it go.

Somebody prodded him in the side. Rhan turned to see the kid who'd been first at the machine.

"What do you think we should do?" he said.

The room had become quiet again. Everybody

seemed to be looking at him.

"Why me?" Rhan said.

The guy shrugged, and coloured.

"Well, you...you know."

And he did. The cafeteria tables of his past. But this time was different, this time they were asking him. The gust swept up through him, and his hesitation fell away like an old coat.

"Okay, let's do it. Let's go talk to him right *now*."

They must have believed him; the room seemed to part, giving them a path out. By the time they hit the hallway they were walking fast and, Rhan realized with a jolt, two had somehow become eight.

"I'm Kent," the guy said.

"I'm — "

"Rhan Van." Kent grinned sheepishly. "Everybody knows you."

If the ceiling had split open to reveal a June sun, Rhan couldn't have been more astonished.

It was only 12:30. The best place to find the principal was probably the staffroom. As they charged up to the second floor Rhan realized that he'd never heard a sound like this, sixteen feet going up a stairwell at the same time.

They gathered outside the staffroom door, puffing faintly. No one else made a move to knock, so Rhan did, three times, loud.

The door opened the width of the music instructor's face.

"Yes?" she said.

"Yeah," Rhan started boldly. "We're a grievance

committee and we're here to meet with Mr. ..."
He stumbled. Oh, God — what was Fly Specks'
real name?!

"Walwryn," Kent supplied at last.

"Mr. Walwryn is having lunch," the music
teacher said.

"Well, we're not," Rhan said cheerfully, "and
that's just what we'd like to talk to him about."

The faintest giggle behind him. The woman's
gaze turned to ice.

"Would you please tell him we're here?" Rhan
pressed.

She closed the door without a word. It seemed
to release a tittering around him, the buoyant
noise of excitement, or nerves.

"Good stuff," Kent whispered. "If he doesn't
show, let's take her as a hostage."

"You take her," Rhan whispered back. "I think
she's a real — "

The door swept open.

"— bag."

Cold, oh, cold. And he got it full force. But the
music teacher had a message.

"Mr. Walwryn will meet with your...*group* in his
office in five minutes," she said.

"Thanks," Rhan said. The door clicked shut in
his face. "Have a nice day."

It broke them up, sent them laughing and talking down the hall. Their noise coming up the stairs
was nothing like the thunder going down. Maybe
that's what being a committee gave you, Rhan
thought. Momentum. Minutes ago they were
strangers standing in the school store. Now they

were something else, hurtling forward.

It crashed in the principal's office. Rhan soon found himself as the "elected" speaker for a group of zombies. And Fly Specks, he discovered, was a lot more at home behind a desk than a microphone.

"I think you'll agree that this was inevitable." Congenial Principal smile. "We were the last school in the district to have vending machines of this type. With the increased concern about nutrition, how could we justify them? We've received several...*numerous* requests from the Parents' Alliance to have them removed. It was your parents who asked for this," the principal stressed.

Not *my* parents, buddy, Rhan thought. But he said, "Nobody is arguing with that. That's not what bothers us."

"Well, what is it, then?"

Rhan glanced left and right. The "committee" seemed to be frozen into position, arms crossed, mouths clamped tight. He took a breath.

"What bothers us is that we weren't consulted." Fly Specks' eyes widened.

"Ever since my first day in this school, all I've heard is 'Take responsibility,' 'Make your own decisions,' 'Act like an adult,'" Rhan hurried on. "And that's okay, this is senior high, right? But then you go and make a decision for us — what we should or shouldn't eat. Well, that's pretty hypocritical, wouldn't you say?"

The principal was taken aback, but he recovered quickly. "We do encourage students to make their own decisions, from the options we provide..."

"And that's the other thing," Rhan cut him off. "This school doesn't provide enough of anything. Have you been in the cafeteria lately? If you can actually get lunch, there's nowhere to sit down and eat it. And the popcorn counter is just as bad. Is it any wonder that we're using the vending machines?"

"A good point," Walwryn said. "An excellent point. And it's something we'll certainly consider in the future. But for the meantime, it's no longer an issue. The machines are gone, and they won't be coming back." He stood up, signalling the end of the meeting. "I thank all of you for your active concern. It's this kind of participation that really makes a difference to a school..."

Panic. Rhan knew he was being put off but he didn't know how to stop it. The moment was slipping from his grasp.

"Perhaps Mr. Van has some suggestions for that future."

The room turned. Sahota was in the open doorway, a clutch of files in his hand. It looked as though he'd been on his way in and had stopped, not wanting to interrupt.

Rhan felt a leap inside. Sahota's expression was as deadpan as always, but Rhan thought he could see something else glimmering there. A hint. It was just what he needed.

"Actually, I do have a few ideas." He turned back to the desk. "Why don't you replace the vending machines with *more* vending machines, you know, the refrigerated kind. Then you could stock sandwiches and stuff, or yoghurt. *Nobody's* going to fight you on yoghurt," he said with a grin. "Or make arrangements for a gut truck..."

"Gut truck?" the principal repeated.

"One of those travelling lunch trucks. They could set up in the parking lot — God, they'd make a fortune."

Fly Specks opened his mouth but he was cut off by the buzzer. Ten to one, four minutes to homeroom. He looked visibly relieved.

"Well, thank you for your active concern," he repeated. "The matter will ... will be taken under advisement."

"Great," Rhan said, grinning. "We'll check back with you."

Sahota stepped aside to let them file out. As Rhan passed, a whisper seemed to curl into his ear. "Bravo."

When the word registered, he turned around in surprise, but by then the office door was closed and they were all out in the hall.

Half the group melted into the flow of kids without a word, but the rest of them hung awkwardly together for a moment.

"Great stuff," Kent said finally. "I think we gave them the message."

Rhan almost laughed. "Yeah, *we* sure did."

"Sorry we jammed out on you," another guy blurted, backing away.

"Well, moral support counts." Rhan shrugged. "They take you more seriously if you're a group."

"Right," Kent said, easing into the crowd. "Well, see you around."

Rhan lifted his hand in a wave, but he was moving now, too. Three minutes to homeroom.

"How can you do that?" said a voice beside him.

He looked. It was a girl, a pretty girl he vaguely remembered as being at the back of their "committee." He'd barely noticed her before. She hadn't said a word until now.

"How do I do what?" Rhan asked.

"I've seen you before. I was in the cafeteria, too, that day." She seemed to be struggling as she walked along beside him. "And like now. How can you just do things, say things? How come you're not embarrassed?"

Rhan was taken aback.

"I don't know," he said.

"Things can be so wrong. Sometimes I could just scream. It's sitting there in my chest and I want to say it, I really do." Her voice wavered. "But I can't. It's like there's these rules and nobody ever says them but they're there."

"You were with us in Walwryn's office," Rhan offered.

She shook her head. "Not really. I was there because *you* were doing all the talking. If somebody had asked me a question, I would have died."

They walked a few steps in silence. Rhan's head was spinning. This day seemed to be changing moment by moment. At every corner he was surprised.

"But you're not like that," the girl continued softly. "You're not like anybody I know. It's as if you dropped in from another planet. How come ... you're not afraid?"

"But I am," he said, and it was the truth. "All the time. It's just that I get madder than I get afraid."

He heard himself and winced. You're babbling, Van. But when he looked at her, he saw she was smiling. She was even prettier when she smiled.

"I like that," the girl said. "It makes sense but it doesn't. Can I use it sometime?"

"You can *have* it," Rhan said.

She stopped outside a door; they had reached her class.

"I might see you around," she said.

"You might," he said.

"Especially if I look." She slipped inside the room.

He stood there, buffeted by kids going in, unaware that he should really move.

The final bell buzzed through his bones, waking him. Rhan turned and started to walk, fast, then faster. Halfway down the hall he broke into a run. He ran as far as the corner and leapt high, a light, breathless jump, his fingertips brushing the ceiling.

FOURTEEN

HE thought about the girl a lot that afternoon. He thought about it all, floated through math and biology like a sleepwalker, but he kept turning back in his mind to look at her, to listen to her.

The rules that nobody says.

Was that it? Rhan wondered. Was that why they'd all been so quiet behind him? For the first time he'd been part of a group, a whole committee gathered together for the same reason, and still he'd been alone. As alone as he'd been on the cafeteria table.

And just as exhilarated. He wasn't sure he'd accomplished much today; he was pretty sure he hadn't. But just to do something! To meet the thing dead on and grab it, for better or worse, seemed more right than sneaking around in the night. Than sabotage.

The word seemed to shake him. He couldn't remember thinking it before. In his mind's eye he could see the superhero wall at Shadowfax; he could see his blue video knight streaking through the maze of tunnels. Sabotage wasn't a word he would have put with either picture.

Maybe that was part of what had been draining him this week. He could almost feel the disapproval from the guys on the wall, as if it came from his own family. And maybe it did. They each had different beginnings — toxic disasters, crumbling planets — but we're the same, Rhan thought. It was a brotherhood, a brotherhood bound by honour and rules.

And maybe he'd been breaking them.

By 3:30 he was flying. The more he thought the faster his mind seemed to go, until he was streaking forward at the speed of light. Blue light.

Rhan dumped his books into his locker. The time had come. He was done with sniping and sneaking and pushing over walls. He'd find Thalie and he'd tell her everything — who he was and how he got that way. He was mad at himself for avoiding her this week. Of all the people in the world he should open up to, she was the one. She was the most like him.

He felt a flare of passion, even love. I'll save you, Rhan thought, but I've got to do it the right way. He was going to confront Garry with the truth, threaten him with exposure, challenge him to a duel if he had to. Anything, as long as it was direct.

Rhan pulled on his jacket as he strode down the hall.

"Congratulations, Mr. Van."

Rhan turned. He'd been walking past the main office, and now he saw Sahota standing in its doorway. He veered over toward him.

"For what?" he said.

"You were most effective today."

Rhan grinned. "You think so?"

"Oh, most certainly. Your committee — did you assemble it yourself?"

"They sort of assembled me."

The corners of Sahota's mouth played with a smile. "Well, the result was most impressive. And highly effective."

That word again. It made Rhan wonder.

"What?" he pressed.

"Well." Sahota hesitated, then tilted his head. Rhan took the cue and followed him into his own office. Sahota eased the door behind them, not shut, but a hand's width open.

"Now this is only a rumour, mind you, and do not say you heard it from me..."

Rhan leaned forward impatiently.

"...but it is my understanding that investigations are already underway into the possible advantages of installing assorted new vending machines."

"Already? I can't believe it. That's great, that's fantastic! That's..." He stumbled. It occurred to him who was probably behind the sudden push. "Thank you," he said, and he meant it. "Thank you very much."

Sahota shook his head. "You identified the problem, Mr. Van, and you presented a solution. The glory of the moment is entirely yours."

Glory. Rhan was grinning again. He liked the way this guy talked.

"Okay," he agreed cheerfully. "I'll take it."

The conversation seemed to be at an end. Rhan started to leave.

"Please," Sahota said suddenly. "Just one more thing."

Rhan turned. The vice-principal looked very uncomfortable leaning against his desk, so uncomfortable that Rhan felt a brief, sudden freeze. He had a haunting sense of the cafeteria doors. Maybe that was the real reason he was in here. Oh, God, was he going to have to worry about that for the rest of his life?

But the vice-principal said, "I'm afraid I have a confession to make. And I want you to know I don't usually do this. To me it seems to be a violation of privacy, to research someone who is not a patient, who hasn't asked for my interest. I prefer to evaluate people from my own experience with them, to know them by how they are, not by what I read."

Rhan was starting to relax. He thought he understood this, what it was, and where it was going.

"But," he prompted.

"But," Sahota agreed. "I must admit you mystified me. You are so persistently unique, Mr. Van. So outspoken, so..."

"Weird?" Rhan supplied.

Sahota smiled. "That's one way of putting it. This," he gestured to include the school, "does nothing to foster individuality. We give no prizes for it, no scholarships. By accident or design the system encourages the herd instinct — or maybe it is only the nature of people. It is so much safer to be lost in the crowd." He sounded suddenly wistful. "The curse of my profession is that you come to remember each year as a particular crowd.

"And then every once in a long while, you see it. The spark. Frustrating, troublesome, and yet so bright you can't keep from looking at it. This time it made me wonder. Where does this come from? How does it survive? And so I began to look..."

There his voice tumbled, as if into a well. After a moment he said, "I am so sorry. Please, accept my condolences. It is a difficult thing, to lose both parents."

The air was very still. Rhan could feel Sahota's shock from across the floor, and yet he was released, somehow. So few people knew this part. He never told it himself. To be in a room where the truth was known — without having had to say it — was a relief.

He wanted Sahota to know that, and that he was all right now. It had been nine years and he was all right.

"Lose both parents," he said lightly. "I could never make sense of that. It makes it sound like I left them at the mall."

He'd meant for Sahota to laugh, or at least smile. But the man only nodded and said nothing. The silence seemed to stretch until it was too big to ignore, an open prairie that called to you to run in it.

"But people have a real problem with words," Rhan said quickly. "Like murder. They call it Domestic Violence — as opposed to that firstclass, *prime time* violence, I guess. How could anybody take 'Domestic Violence' seriously? It sounds like cows and sheep pushing each other around."

Faster and faster, running in that field. He could hear himself, rapid fire, each word sharpening itself on the one before. Oh, God, he didn't mean to do this. He didn't mean to do it but he couldn't stop.

"So if Domestic Violence isn't real violence,

then domestic murder isn't the real thing, either. Isn't that a relief! There's less paperwork if you don't have to change the laws. And my father had the decency to kill himself, too — saved taxpayers the cost of a trial and all those years in jail. That was big of him, don't you think? When you get right down to it, he was probably a *prince* of a guy — "

"Rhan."

The word like a shake, or a hand on his arm. It stopped him, finally.

"Please tell me what you're telling me," Sahota said quietly, just a trace of doctor in his voice.

Rhan's heart was still thudding in his throat, so hard he felt dizzy. Where he'd meant to go with this and where he'd actually gone were two different places.

"I'm just telling you," he started. "I'm just telling you — don't be sorry. It's okay. There are lots of guys whose parents up and die on them — Batman, Superman, the Wolverine." He tried to grin but his face was wood. "It's kind of a club. The price of admission is real steep, but you only have to pay it once."

And then he bowed, the stiff little tilt that was Sahota's bow. And then he left.

Out in the hall again, heading toward the exit. He had to lean forward to keep moving, as if into the thrust of a storm. The urge to give up and sit down in the middle of the polished floor was very strong.

Don't look. Keep going. It's all right.

At the doors the gale seemed to die abruptly, or

he had reached its eye. With relief he pushed his way out.

And there she was. Leaning against the stone wall of the school, looking the other way, but she was *there*. He hadn't been looking for proof, but his chest flooded with warmth. They were synchronized, connected somehow. This was meant to be.

Rhan bounded over and caught her arm, tugging her around. "Hi!"

Her eyes made him drop his hand.

"Oh, it's you," Thalie said. "What do you want now?"

"I...I want to talk."

"Oh, really? Well, it took you a whole week to make that Big Decision. I thought you'd forgotten who I was. If you wanted to talk so badly, there are things called telephones, you know. I imagine you've got one."

Rhan's defenses rushed up. "And so do you," he shot back. "You could have called me."

"Maybe I was hoping...you'd be different. Maybe I was just giving you the chance. I should have known. You're all the same, once you get what you want."

The memory pressed itself on him suddenly, the close, dark air of the playground tunnel, skin on skin, his own breath like a drowning man. He hadn't known there were rules attached to that, too.

Thalie had started to walk away, her chin set. Rhan hurried to catch up and fell in step, his hands dug deep into the pockets of his jacket.

"I'm sorry I didn't call," he said. "I've had a bad week."

"Oh, *really*?" But then she paused, as if waiting for him to tell her. All the other things he'd planned to say were still there, burning in his chest, but they were stuck, somehow. When he opened his mouth, he chickened out.

"I have to move," he said.

She listened impatiently while he told her about Eldorado, and how he and Gran earned a living, and why they couldn't just move anywhere.

"Well, it's too bad," Thalie said, with an edge in her voice. "But it's not like you're leaving the planet. We can bus it if we have to. And besides, lots of worse things happen to people. Maybe you're getting this experience to widen your perspective."

"Sure, like a groundhog gets widened — on the highway," he snapped.

"Can't you ever be serious!"

"And can't you have a little sympathy?"

"What do you want from me? I've had to move lots of times — and nobody ever asks me how I feel about it. They just do it." Her voice seemed to drop. "Maybe I've had a bad week, too," she said quietly.

She could do it, this girl. Make him so mad one minute, and then pull his heart up into his throat.

"What happened?" Rhan asked.

For a few seconds she just walked, watching the pavement in front of her feet.

"I told him," she said.

"What? Who?"

"Garry. I told him it was us...who did the house on Belmont."

A hammer in his ears. "Are you crazy?" he whispered. He grabbed her by the shoulders, so hard it scared him. "Are you crazy!"

She wrenched away. "It was necessary," she said angrily. "You don't understand."

"You're right — I don't. Explain it to me. Explain why it's necessary that I face criminal charges!"

"He had to know what bit him. I couldn't have him thinking it was a random act of vandalism. He had to know," she stressed every word, "why he was being punished."

The world had begun to sway. Rhan leaned against a metal bus stop pole. His decision to be direct, to meet things head on, seemed to disintegrate. His prosecution would kill Gran, was all he could think.

Thalie was tugging on his arm. "Will you stop overreacting and just listen to me! He's not going to press charges."

Rhan looked up. "And why not?"

"I've told you before. He doesn't take me seriously, not even when it costs him money," she said bitterly. "Look, it's been almost a week, and the police haven't surrounded your house, have they?"

"No."

"Well, there's the proof for you. Nothing touches him. No matter what I do, he doesn't... he..."

And she burst into tears.

FIFTEEN

THEY sat on a bus bench for a long time. Buses pulled up and slowed, but one clear look from Rhan and the driver kept right on going.

Thalie didn't look up. She stared at the bedraggled tissue she was twisting in her hands, wringing until it was in damp shreds. Rhan had never noticed before that she had almost no fingernails, how they were bitten or broken until there was no white.

"I just thought that if he suffered some kind of consequences, it would make a difference," Thalie said. "His problem is that he never has opposition. My mother encourages him — this whole greed-based society encourages him. No wonder he doesn't know right from wrong."

Rhan blinked. She was making excuses for the Dark Lord?

"I just thought that if somebody made him stop and think about what he was doing, he would change," Thalie finished. "He could reform."

"But how can you even worry about somebody who...hurt you," Rhan said angrily.

Thalie hesitated. "Isn't the whole issue about Good being better than Evil? I mean, if you were in a war and you caught one of the enemy, would you shoot to kill, or would you maybe just wound him? If you shot him in the leg, you'd have the chance to convince him to join your side."

Shooting to wound. It was not something he understood. Or his family.

"And even if you couldn't convince him," Thalie continued, "at least he'd be in pain."

Another bus rolled up and this one did stop, letting people off. One woman gave Rhan a look, as if he was the reason for Thalie's teary face.

A short, ragged breath beside him made him turn back.

"Well." Thalie swallowed, composing herself. "It's over, anyway. I tried my hardest and I didn't change...anything. I tried my hardest and I still lost. They're getting married," she said. "He's even building her a new house."

Over. Lost. Those were the words that registered. And after the surprise came the panic — a trickle, then a fountain, then a geyser.

"It can't be over," he blurted.

"I give up," Thalie said. "It's finished."

"But it can't be!"

"And why not?" She was getting angry at him now.

Because I haven't won yet.

"Look," he said, "those Underground people you think were so great, that Resistance. You think they gave up easy? The first bridge that didn't blow — they packed up and sold the dynamite?"

Her eyes flashed. "They had an important cause. They knew they were fighting an enormous evil —"

"Isn't all evil enormous?" Rhan said.

"But nothing I do touches him!"

"Then we just haven't hit the thing he cares about," Rhan said.

She seemed to flinch, as if he had struck her,

140

but he couldn't stop. He could hear his heart, like footsteps running, running down a long, empty corridor. *Don't look. Keep going.*

"Everybody cares about something," Rhan pushed. "And that's what you go after. The nerve. It isn't nice, but — "

"All's fair in love and war," Thalie said. Her face was cooling, hardening, fire turning to ice. "You're right," she continued. "You're absolutely right. We didn't hit the thing he cares about. But I know what it is, and I know what to do."

And she told him. And he felt the disbelief wash over him in a slow-motion wave, because this was so far from him. This was so far from something he could do. Wasn't it?

One level and one level and one level more.

Wasn't it?

Suddenly Thalie was standing, and she smiled, a little sad, but very determined.

"I know we can do this," she whispered. "I know we can do this together. I'll meet you tonight."

She reached out as if to touch his hair, then leaned in suddenly and kissed him. And she was gone before he realized he hadn't kissed her back. Or said no.

The afternoon and early evening passed like pieces of a dream. Rhan kept moving, afraid to stop, as if there was something on his heels. He remembered standing outside the Rite Shop like a tourist, wanting to go in, needing to, but unable to propel himself through the doors. He remembered phoning Gran from a phone booth, one ear full of traffic and the other full of her terse worry. He was sorry he was late, he was sorry he'd missed supper.

"Well, don't be," she said finally, exasperated. "Just get home. There's...there's something we have to talk about."

"I'm sorry," Rhan said, and he hung up.

He remembered walking, one foot determinedly leading the other in a haphazard trail of sidewalks. When he found himself on Darryl's street, dangerously close to Darryl's house, he reined himself up sharp.

No. He wouldn't understand.

But he didn't know if *he* understood. He'd made some big speeches inside his head today, about winning the right way, about a brotherhood of honour. But now when he looked into his heart, he realized they weren't nearly as big as the other thing.

I'm gonna get you, Dark Lord. I'm gonna get you any way I can.

He knew he'd led Thalie into this. The mechanics of the plan belonged to her, the what and when and how, but he'd been behind her, pushing. Rhan didn't make excuses for the Dark Lord; he wouldn't shoot to wound. Because he knew first hand something that Thalie didn't, that evil left alone didn't go away. It grew, it devoured, it triumphed.

But not this time.

SIXTEEN

THE windows at Thalie's house were all dark now. Rhan didn't know the exact time but he could feel how late it was. The whole street was quiet, the deep silence of people in bed, televisions off; so quiet he could hear the faint buzzing of the streetlights overhead. He stationed himself across the road, settled down to wait, but in a very few minutes her front door eased open a crack. Rhan hurried over.

"I'll go open the garage," Thalie said. "You stand here and watch that window." She pointed to the second storey. "It's their bedroom. If the lights come on, you signal me."

"And then what?" Rhan asked.

"I'll hurry."

She closed the door again and he glued his eyes to the big double windows on the second floor. It could all stop here, here and now. He felt a sudden clutch inside him, but he wouldn't let himself decide whether the thought was relief or disappointment.

Don't look. Keep going.

The sudden, slow chugging of the electric door made him catch his breath — it seemed as loud as a bulldozer — but the window stayed dark. A miracle.

He heard his name in a terse whisper, and he peered into the dim garage. Thalie had tugged the tarp off the old Harley and was motioning him inside.

He knew about this part, knew it was necessary,

and yet the sight of glinting chrome and metal seemed to hit him in the chest. Garry's baby was bigger than he remembered. It was more real.

"You're sure you can drive it?" he asked softly.

"Yes."

"Do you have a licence?"

"No."

Thalie was rummaging in a corner of the garage, behind a cluster of boxes. She lifted out a jerrycan and handed it to him. From the weight he could tell it was full.

She took hold of the handlebars and released the kickstand, but didn't mount the bike.

"I'm going to cruise it to the end of the block," she said. "Less noise. We'll start from there. I don't have a remote so you're going to have to hit the switch and get out before the door closes."

Rhan hesitated.

"Yes or no," Thalie said.

He'd said that, hadn't he, in front of the school a long time ago. How strange your own words could sound, when they finally boomeranged back at you.

Rhan took a breath. "Let's do it," he said.

Thalie backed the bike carefully out of the garage, then swivelled it so the nose was aimed at the street. With one expert move she straddled it and coasted down the driveway onto the asphalt, letting gravity carry her forward. Someone had taught her this. She seemed to have that cool ease about everything now. They'd only thought this up a few hours ago. How could she be so...prepared?

He couldn't see her, but he heard the gutsy

rumble as she kicked the bike to life. She was ready now, waiting. Rhan hit the wall switch and shot forward. The door wasn't fast but it was coming down. He managed to duck under at waist level, the jerrycan sloshing as he sprinted into the street.

At the end of the block, he slid awkwardly onto the long leather seat behind her, heart thumping, and cradled the can between his legs for safekeeping. He was wondering if she really knew how to drive this thing.

He glanced back up the sidewalk the way they'd come, and froze. A light. A second-storey light. Was it from her house?

"Hey!" he shouted into her ear.

"Hang on!" Thalie called back.

The bike catapulted forward and he grabbed her waist to keep from flying. It was two blocks before he remembered to breathe.

Lights, buildings seemed to blur past at supernatural speed, yet he knew she wasn't going fast enough to arouse suspicion.

When they stopped at traffic lights, they received only the barest glance from the drivers beside them. This was a city where two kids riding a motorcycle after midnight didn't matter to anyone.

Hanging on, he could feel her move with the bike, shifting gears, shoulder-checking as she weaved through traffic. The closeness reminded him of hiding from the janitor at Bedford, not being in the tunnels at the park.

The old bike roared on and on, through the city

to the suburbs and finally beyond, to the wilderness where monsters grew.

The vibrating rumble seemed to stay in his body even after she'd cut the engine. Rhan dismounted and peered down the rough road behind them. He listened, ears straining for the well-oiled purr that he knew could be so soft. But moments passed, and there was nothing.

Okay. Deep breath. *All right.*

Turning back he saw that Thalie had already started toward the structure, jaw set as she picked her way over loose boards, trying to stay out of the muck.

Rhan guessed that all new developments started out like this: everything green had been scraped away to a flat surface, or gouged out into basements. The board frames and half-built houses were separated by vast spaces, empty lots where building hadn't begun. In between, heavy machines had torn up the charcoal-grey dirt, leaving trails full of rainwater. It was hard to imagine that people would live here — and soon — but he knew they would. This would be a neighbourhood like any other, like his own.

He felt one more jab of conscience, that he'd renounced sabotage and taken it up again, all in the same day. But he was through arguing with himself; the poke only made him mad now.

You made your decision. Just stick to it, for Christ's sake!

Rhan turned and stormed through the muck to Garry's new house.

Money, or money to come, that's what this was.

It was meant to be the biggest house on the street, and so far it was the most finished. Two storeys with outer walls, and then a third floor sketched out in framework, still open to the sky.

And that's where Thalie had got to.

"Don't forget!" she called down to him.

"Who was your slave last week," he grumbled irritably, but he had forgotten the jerrycan, and went back to get it.

Once inside, he realized how treacherous a half-finished house could be. With only dim moonlight through the bare windows, he stumbled over forgotten tools and boards, cursing. On the second level he made another discovery. Instead of stairs, there was only a square cut in the ceiling. How the hell was he supposed to get to the top?!

He called her name, not nicely.

"What?" she called back, peering down at him.

"Am I supposed to fly up or what?"

"Didn't you see the ladder on top of the garage? Go out that window; it's right there."

Oh, great, he thought, ducking his head as he crawled out. Garage roofs and ladders. One-handed yet, carrying a flammable liquid. That's what she'd brought him for.

Yet in the same instant, he knew she hadn't brought him at all.

On the top floor, the sense of height and sky made him dizzy. He grabbed a wall stud to steady himself. Thalie strode over.

"Okay," she said briskly, taking the jerrycan from him. "Start gathering wood pieces and shavings, anything small that'll burn well. The wood's wet up here from all the rain. We have to create hot spots to help it catch."

Rhan set to work, relieved to have a specific task. But as he watched Thalie pour gasoline on the piles, a question sprang out.

"Why are we starting at the top? Doesn't fire burn up?"

"We can't take any chances," she said evenly. "We have to prepare each floor so it will all go. I don't want anything left to rebuild." She moved to the next heap and began to soak it. "It's her house, he's building it for her. After the wedding he was going to move us all over. Well," she finished, "we'll just see about that."

"Little children shouldn't play with fire."

Thalie and Rhan whipped around. Garry was standing on the ladder, leaning in, his chest level with the floor.

Rhan's mind bolted ahead. How had he driven up without them hearing? Had he gotten here first, somehow, and been hiding in the unlit development?

But it didn't really matter now. With one powerful move, the Dark Lord pulled himself up and onto the floorboards of the third level.

For an instant there was no sound. His glance brushed over Rhan before it swept in on her.

"Give me the matches, Thalie."

She didn't move. Her eyes were still wide with surprise. Garry took a step.

"I said give me the matches."

Like falling into a dream, Rhan lunged, scooping up a length of wood the size of a baseball bat.

And then he was in Garry's path.

The man stepped back. It was his turn to be surprised. But he struggled for his cool and managed to pull it up one more time.

"We meet in the strangest places, dude."

Rhan's heart was pounding. He could see his weapon tremble, just a bit. He had it in two hands in front of him, the way he'd hold a sword, the sharp edges digging into his hands. But it did not feel strange. It suddenly seemed that it had been coming to this from the very first moment.

"Turn around," Rhan said. "Go home."

"Jesus Christ! I'm not going to let her burn down the house!"

Rhan took a step.

"Turn around," he said again. He wasn't taller than Garry but it seemed that he was looking down on his head, on his skull, every nerve screaming I will, I will, I don't want to but I will...

And Garry knew it, too. Panic was beginning to peel him away, the calm surface rippling like old paint.

"You don't know anything! This doesn't concern you —" His bravado stumbled. "Look, I made a mistake, *once*..."

"A mistake!" Thalie's voice rang out behind Rhan. "Loving me is a mistake?!"

"I never said I loved you."

"Liar." Her voice trembled. "You did and you still do. Admit it!"

Love. The word seemed to buffet Rhan. It struck him on the side of the head, then again.

Garry was looking into Rhan's face, pleading.

"I just made a mistake and I knew it, and I tried to make it stop. But she wouldn't let it. For the past two months it's been 'meet me, drive me, be with me — or else.' I...I couldn't have Lei knowing."

"No, not your precious Lei," Thalie continued bitterly. "She applauds you, encourages you, but I'm worse than a conscience, aren't I? I see things and I'm not afraid to speak up. That's why you chose *her* — she makes it so easy. Someone to sink to the bottom with."

"Do you see?" Garry said to Rhan. "It doesn't matter what I say, what I want."

"If you would just listen to reason," Thalie called. "Together we could have done so much! I have the ideas, the spirit, I know what needs to be done. And you have the resources to build it. We'd be doing things for humanity, not for greed. If you'd just listen to your heart, you'd know that I'm the one, not her."

"Do you see?" Garry said.

And Rhan saw. He saw that he was a fool. A fucking mortal fool.

He spun around, and hurled the length of wood. It hit a wall stud with a *crack* that vibrated the floorboards.

"You lied to me," he cried. "You made me think you were in trouble, that you needed help. You used me!"

"Used you?" Thalie shot back. "You were the one who pushed yourself on me. I didn't want your help and I told you so. I told you that very first night. No, you were so bound and determined to...to...God, I don't even know what. You never

150

even asked me what was wrong."

His cheeks were stinging. He thought he'd been sparing her, staying away from sacred ground.

"But you seemed to understand things," Thalie continued, her voice softening. "When I saw you on that table at school, I thought you were someone who could feel things, believe in things. And when you wanted to be my comrade, I was so glad! Because then I wouldn't have to fight this evil alone."

Comrade. Rhan was pierced. Is that what he was to her? And yet he could see in her face that she believed it. Except one of them had only been shooting to wound.

This was crazy! The things he'd done for her, the risks he'd taken, and she wasn't even functioning in reality. All this, and she was somewhere else.

And where are you? The words crawled over him like a chill. Who are you fighting?

Then he could feel it, the breeze from an open door on his back, air moving over the stone floor. He was still trapped in the castle corridors, fighting his way through the tunnels. If he turned around fast enough he would see the real Dark Lord, safe in hell, laughing at him.

But he didn't turn around.

A ragged sigh made him look to his left. Garry was leaning against the framework, staring out on the dark development.

"She calls me evil," he said quietly. "Well, how evil is terrorism, or blackmail? What do you call someone who makes me feel guilty every time I kiss the woman I love?"

"NO!" A shrill cry of despair. Garry seemed to flinch, but he kept his back to her.

"Yes," he said. "I love Lei, and I'll marry her, if she can still stand me after I tell her the truth. But one way or another, this nightmare is going to end tonight."

There was no warning to what happened next. When Rhan saw Thalie she was already moving, an angry blur charging across the plank floor. It was too late to intercept. As she hit Garry Rhan lunged, a raw, animal leap of instinct. And he caught hold just as the man went over the edge.

The world was a tunnel. It was his own arm, and the startled, stricken face like a white blot at the end of a black tube. The whole world was his grip on 160 pounds.

There was no pain; he wasn't even aware that there should be. Without effort, it seemed, he lifted Garry out of the abyss and pulled him onto the floorboards.

For minutes they just sat, panting, staring at each other. They both knew he couldn't have done what he just did.

"You saved my life, dude," Garry said finally.

"Don't call me dude."

The throaty roar of the old Harley brought them both to their feet. Hanging onto the open framework, Rhan watched Thalie zoom away, a streak of chrome on a dark road. His heart sank to his runners. When he looked at Garry, the man shook his head.

"No. I won't chase her down this time. It's part of the game, too, and I'm not playing anymore."

He leaned his forehead against a wooden beam. "I have to go wake somebody up now," he said softly.

They began the descent from the tower.

Garry was upset that Rhan wouldn't get in the car.

"I can't just leave you here," he said.

"I'm not staying."

"It's two in the morning. Isn't somebody worried about you?"

"Probably," Rhan said.

Garry ran his hand through his hair, stalling, finding words. "I'm sorry you got sucked into this mess. Maybe, well, maybe I was hoping she'd fall for you, get me off the hook." He hesitated. "I know you think I'm the jerk in all of this."

"No, you're only *a* jerk, not *the* jerk." Rhan could barely hear his own voice. "And I didn't get sucked in, I jumped."

Garry seemed to be studying a distant garage. "Were you really going to...hit me?"

Rhan didn't answer. He turned away and started to walk. In a few minutes the silver car passed him, and the relief was so sudden and so great he stumbled, and almost fell. But somehow his two old friends, the quiet and the dark, slipped their arms around him and held him up as he trudged along the rough road home.

SEVENTEEN

HE got his first pair of glasses the summer he was nine. He would never forget that, sitting in the optometrist's chair with the lights out, peering into the double barrels of the equipment, the doctor's steady voice very near his right ear, but disembodied in the dark.

"Just tell me, every time I click the lens, is it better or worse?"

The black-and-white images clicking in and out of focus, what he thought was clear becoming even clearer, or blurring away. The sound of his own voice, over and over and over until he was bored and dizzy and not even sure if he was telling the truth.

Better. Better. Worse. Better. Worse.

How long it took to pick the frames in the tiny shop next door, Gran suspicious and hesitant about anything that came with a guarantee. The display said, 'Can't Break 'Em'; each cowhide carrying case said, 'Can't Break 'Em,' and still she didn't believe.

"Well, he's a *boy*, you know," she said.

The clerk said the manufacturer knew boys, that the frames were designed *especially* for boys.

Then Gran said the manufacturer didn't know this particular boy, and the clerk said, Lady, you'd have to drive over these glasses with a truck. And Gran turned to him suddenly and said, "Just don't you get run over by a truck!"

He would never forget the day he wore them home, the strange weight on his face, the 'Can't

Break 'Em' cowhide case growing sweaty in his hand. If Gran spoke, he didn't know it. If the bus was hot, he didn't feel it. Rhan was mesmerized by the leaves on trees, the grill of a car, the profile of a girl across the aisle. Nobody told him it was supposed to be like this. Black-and-white letters through the optometrist's lens — that wasn't the world. The world had texture; it was intricate, fascinating, beautiful. And nobody had told him!

The bus bounced along and Rhan bounced with it, unable to speak. He knew he should be grateful and he was. But still he couldn't stop the betrayal from tightening in his body like a cramp.

•

Friday Rhan awoke to the pain. Shoulders, back, legs. Every part he had used in the rescue of Garry, or the long walk home, was gripped by an angry ache. His mortal failings had caught up to him with a vengeance.

It was a full minute before it occurred to him that the house was too quiet, and the light was all wrong for morning.

He hoisted himself up on an elbow and squinted at the clock radio: two-thirteen.

Two-thirteen.

"Jesus Christ!" He threw back the covers and swung his legs over the edge, panic overtaking pain. His thoughts raced as he pulled on his pants. Why had Gran let him sleep? Had he been too hard to wake up, or...or...

He burst out of his room, shirtless.

His grandmother was on the floor beside an

open cardboard box, packing clothes.

"Well, good morning, Bonnie Prince Charles," she said crisply, without looking up.

Rhan sagged in the doorway with both relief and dread. How much trouble was he in for? Well, the condemned always got a last cigarette, didn't they? He backed into his room for one he had squirreled away, and put on his glasses. He lit up and braced himself.

Take it like a man, he told himself.

But when he stepped into the living-room this time, he could see. And he saw that the clothes she was packing were his. Oh, God, she was true to her word. She was throwing him out!

The man lost it. He dropped to the floor at his grandmother's feet and begged for another chance. In silence she listened to him ramble, then finally she said, "It's going to cost you."

"How much?"

"The truth."

Rhan sucked in his breath. That much.

The story came out in pieces, and not in the right order, and certainly the edited-for-grandmother version.

"I was just trying to help her, you know," he said, staring at the long ash of his cigarette. "Or that's what I thought I was doing."

"Do you think maybe you've learned something here?"

"Don't turn this into a TV show, okay?" Rhan said softly. He tipped the ash onto his jeans and rubbed it into the fabric. They needed washing anyway.

"It's just the truth," he said.

"I know."

"What?" Rhan looked up.

"A lady phoned here this morning looking for her daughter. Told me how you got yourself right into the middle of a family row, and now the girl's run off. Well, it was a blow, you know. We all like to think our kids know when to back away from a bad situation. But somehow I wasn't really surprised."

Thalie was missing. Rhan felt the news in a thud. But he wasn't surprised, either.

"She left this phone number," Gran said, reaching for a scrap on the coffee table. "You're to call her — and only her — if you see the girl."

He took the paper. In the back of his mind he registered that it wasn't an exchange for this district of the city. Lei was somewhere else now.

"Anyhow, it was lots to think about," Gran continued. "That's why I let you sleep."

Rhan stood up angrily. "You mean you weren't going to throw me out?"

"No."

He thunked the box with his foot. "Then what the hell's this all about?"

"Watch your mouth," she snapped. "You're talking to an old lady."

Then Gran told her story, the one she'd wanted him to come home for the night before. She'd found a place for them to move to: Thunder Bay, Ontario. Population 116,000.

"We'll move in with my cousin Zoe for awhile, but it's not permanent or nothing," Gran insisted.

"It's just 'til we get back on our feet."

"You never said you had a cousin Zoe," Rhan said.

"Well, I hate her guts."

"Then why are we moving there?"

Gran looked shocked. "She's *family*."

Rhan was going through a bit of shock himself. "Thunder Bay," he repeated numbly. "It snows there, doesn't it? Christ, what'd I ever do to you?"

"Give yourself time," Gran said drily. "It'll come to you."

They spent the rest of the day and most of the weekend sorting through their possessions, deciding what was for the trip and what was for the dump.

"What about the couch and the table and stuff?" Rhan asked.

"Well, it was a furnished place."

"You mean all this belongs to *him*?"

Gran nodded.

Rhan glanced around the suite. "Thank God," he said.

Gran told him to be ruthless and thorough, and he was. He dug through his closet and drawers and filled up garbage bags like a man possessed. It was a relief to have something to do.

It was night that was hard. Lying in his bed, waiting for sleep that wouldn't come. They might have found her by now, but he doubted it. Thalie, he realized, was a very determined victim.

He could see where she got that steel. Lei's new phone number was still folded up in the pocket of his jeans. In his mind's eye he could see Garry wandering around his big house alone. Maybe the man hadn't gotten away with anything.

He'd been so worried that he would. It frightened him just to remember how he'd wanted to crush Garry, burn his house, bring the wood crashing down on his head. How he'd wanted to destroy him and make everything right, this time.

There was nothing noble about that kind of justice. It didn't make him feel like a super anything. It made him feel like shit.

He draped his arm over his acid eyes.

RanVan was dead. If someone who had never lived could die. And he would believe it, he would accept it.

But as the warm haze of sleep was finally wrapping him up, he realized there was one part of that night he couldn't explain. He knew he couldn't lift 160 pounds.

Adrenalin, he told himself. That was how he'd caught Garry, saved him.

But adrenalin wasn't electric blue.

•

"Look what I found," Gran said Sunday afternoon. Rhan took the big box from her and opened the panels of the lid. He pulled out a brown cowboy hat with a plastic whistle, a pirate's patch and spotted shirt. He knew what was underneath, the cape and mask at the bottom of the box.

"Your costumes," Gran said brightly. "Birthday suits."

He started shoving things back in. "Yeah, well, they don't fit anymore."

"But they're still good." Gran put the cowboy hat on her head.

"Chuck 'em," he said thickly, forcing the box back into her hands. He went into his room and stayed there for a long time.

Monday was October 30th. Gran woke him up early for school.

"But it's my birthday *eve*," Rhan complained. "And we leave tonight anyway. How much learning can they cram into my brain in one day?"

"Get out of that bed or *I'm* going to cram something into your brain," she grumbled.

Rhan sighed. They usually had this argument on his birthday, and he always lost. When he was living on his own, he decided, he was going to celebrate his whole birthday *week*.

Gran had phoned the school office on Friday to advise them of the move, but Rhan found he had to explain it again to each individual teacher. He got pretty tired of the question, "Thunder *what*?"

"And lightning!" he finally snapped in Psychology. "It's Inuit for 'study your geography.'"

He would have been ejected from the class but the final bell rang, and he fled into the hall with relief. Teachers in Thunder Bay might not be any better, he thought, but they couldn't possibly be any worse.

"Good afternoon, Mr. Van. What a fortuitous coincidence."

Rhan grinned suddenly, in spite of his mood. "We seem to have a lot of coincidences," he said. "Do you study my class schedule, or what?"

"Good luck," Sahota said in his gravest tones,

"is always skilfully engineered."

They walked a few steps in silence.

"You are leaving us," Sahota said.

"Yeah, but don't take it personally."

"I have been contemplating how the mood of this school will be affected by your absence," Sahota said. "Why, the very ambiance of the institution hangs by a thread. I anticipate a frenzied return to ..."

"Normal?" Rhan supplied.

"Dreadfully so."

Rhan walked, feeling the guilt rising inside him, running to the surface, again.

"There's something I have to tell you," he said, staring straight ahead. "About the cafeteria..."

Sahota cut him off. "There is no need."

"I want you to know I didn't do it."

"But you were there."

Rhan felt a slight tingle crawl up the back of his neck. "Yeah. Yeah, I was. How did you know?"

They had arrived at Rhan's locker, but he didn't move to open it.

"I do not think we are aware of the mark, the imprint we leave on all that we touch," Sahota said finally, quietly. "One part of the event required intelligence, the other only anger. Your signature, Mr. Van, is a neon light." He raised his hand in a benediction, or a prophesy. "Go forth," he whispered, "and illuminate."

Rhan watched him leave, straight shoulders, hands clasped behind his back. He looked and looked, the tingle still running up his neck and over his scalp, a little like awe.

When he opened his locker, a paper fluttered to the floor. It had been pushed in through the crack in the door. He stooped to pick it up.

Arachnaman was in full flight, frozen in one of his heroic leaps, his mighty spider's body straining forward, his deadly fangs glistening. Rhan knew this image so well, and yet it caught him fresh, the fluid black strokes against the white paper. It was just so *good*, he thought. He wondered again if Darryl knew that.

There were no words, no thought balloon. That had always been his part. But this time it didn't matter. He knew this was goodbye.

Rhan folded the drawing carefully and put it in his pocket. It had been a hard lesson, discovering that imagining and believing weren't the same thing. But that didn't mean they weren't close. He would miss Arachnaman.

Rhan cleaned out his locker and turned in his textbooks at the front office. He was amazed when they refunded his deposit out of petty cash. He staggered out, reeling with wealth. He'd forgotten how much books cost. There was ten hours' worth of rug-cleaning here! First he'd buy a pack of cigarettes — hell, he'd buy two. Then he'd sit down with Stormers and he'd play it until he *beat* the bugger. His heart leapt at the thought. Would he have enough time, enough money? Had anybody ever beat it? What if he was the first?

He walked down the school steps into the courtyard, dizzy with optimism.

No, please, no photographs. The cover of Time? *Oh, well, maybe just one.* Flash! Flash! *And remem-*

ber, kids, don't try this on your video games at home...

Rhan stopped. He'd been working so hard at not thinking about Thalie, but now she was dead ahead, a streak of black on the other side of the chainlink fence. She was nowhere near an opening so he started straight to her, afraid she'd disappear in the time it would take him to go around.

Thalie looked like someone who'd been away from home for three days. Her makeup was long gone, cried away or worn off, and the skin stretched over her features made him think of parcel paper. Her eyes were too bright, not from tears but something else. He wondered when she'd eaten last.

Rhan curled his fingers through the fence.

"I...I can't stay," Thalie said. "I think they're looking for me."

Rhan nodded numbly. In one part of his brain he was jumping up and down, the alarms shrieking. Another part of him was very still.

She leaned closer. "I have another idea," she whispered. "And I know it'll work but I need your help."

"What is it?" he said.

Thalie looked over her shoulder. "Not here, it's too dangerous. I'll meet you tonight and explain everything. Eight o'clock at the park, in the tunnels."

When he didn't reply, the panic seemed to rise in her eyes. She put her hands over his, her flat palms pinning his curled fingers.

"You're the only one I can trust," she pleaded. "You will help me, won't you?"

Guts clenching, knotting. "Yes."

The fear eased away from her face. "All right, I'll see you then."

"Wait." He extricated his hand and dug in his pocket for the fresh roll. He peeled half away and pushed it through the fence at her. Thalie's eyes narrowed as she looked at the money, and then at him, but she didn't reach for it.

He shrugged to take the tension out of his voice. "Get...get some dinner," he said. And breakfast. And lunch.

"I will see you tonight," she insisted. "You will help me."

Rhan took a breath. "I'll help you," he said.

Thalie finally took the money and began to back away. Suddenly she stepped up to the fence again, close, her lips to an opening in the wire.

Kissing her then was the hardest thing he'd done.

Gran wasn't home when he arrived at the suite. Rhan knew she was downtown, getting back the deposit on the utilities. He was glad. He didn't need anyone to see this.

He cleared a path through the boxes and heaps of laundry to the phone. He sat down and dialed.

"I've seen her," he told Lei.

Her relief was frantic, a mother's relief. Did he know where she was now?

"No, but I know where she's going to be."

He told Lei about the tunnels at the park, and then he hung up. And then his glasses tumbled to the floor as his hands slid up under them.

EIGHTEEN

THERE was no sound in the world like the run of a coin down the metal alley, Rhan thought, the dull clink as it dropped onto the pile. And it didn't matter how many coins had run before it, or if all of them had been yours. Each time was a new time, hopeful and bright, money whispering Maybe, maybe, all the way down.

Clink.

Okay, Noble-but-Stupid, show me what you've got. It's your turn to pay off, after all I've paid into you.

It was ten o'clock, and Rhan had been at the Rite Shop since a quarter to eight. He'd come in desperately looking for a world to get lost in, somewhere to be that wasn't the tunnels at the park. He'd hoped to be distracted, but he'd never expected to be so utterly caught up again, hammering the controls, his behind growing numb on the edge of the seat.

He wasn't doing especially well. Skills he'd had when he played every day were rusty now; he found himself making old mistakes. But the sound of it! The look and the feel of it, urging him on through one level and one level and one level more. So he couldn't beat this thing. So it was rigged. He wasn't broke yet, and there was still more than an hour before he and Gran had to leave for the bus depot. He'd spend it how he wanted.

He tried to play smart, not mad, blasting only the gremlins that were a direct threat. *Live another day, insect. I've gotta run.*

The ninth level took him by surprise; he hadn't

been here in a long time. The tenth level was even more of a shock. He'd never been here at all. The little knight stumbled forward, trying to keep his head clear, remember the moves that had got him this far.

Don't panic, metal man. You know this. Clear the path but keep going. You don't know how much time you've got.

Eleventh level. At the very edge of his consciousness he heard the tinkle of Fil's door chime, but he didn't dare lift his eyes from the screen. He was on the doorstep of the Dark Lord and his heart was pounding.

Flying gremlins with blowtorches. No problem. The lava wheel. No problem. It occurred to him that all the attackers and pitfalls were from previous levels — coming faster, closer together, but familiar.

And suddenly, there he was. With his great, flowing cape and three-cornered hat. The knight was astonished. The Dark Lord was barely taller than him. Someone this awful should be bigger, he should fill the whole screen.

Rhan gripped the controls, preparing to shoot, but voices were rising in the corner of the store. He felt a tug of alarm the same moment he fired, and missed. Damn! He dodged the Dark Lord's return bolt of red laser and was lining up for another shot at him.

This time, this time. I'm gonna take you down once and for all...

"I said *now*, old man!"

The voice pulled Rhan out of the game and to his feet. He peered over the shelves toward the front of the store.

And then he realized robbery number eight was in progress.

The thief was burly, and drunk. Rhan could see that even from this distance. How the enormous shoulders swayed unsteadily as he stood in front of the till. He was drunk enough that Fil was resisting. Rhan couldn't make out the words but the storekeeper's gestures were clear: I don't have anything. Get out of here.

Suddenly the man lunged, caught hold of Fil's neck and yanked his head to the counter. But the effort twisted his body and for the first time Rhan could see he had something in his hand. Something with a blade.

And in the time it took for the shock to travel from his heart to his toes, he reached and grabbed and jumped and threw.

Thunk.

The can of Chunky Chicken caught the thief at the base of his skull, driving him forward, whamming his face onto the counter. For a second he seemed to hover, as if he was going to straighten up, but then he slumped and slid to the floor, releasing his grip on Fil and the hunting knife at the same time.

Fil stared, wide-eyed, at the man on the floor. Then he looked up at Rhan.

"Holy shit," he whispered.

•

"Show me," the constable said.

Rhan sighed. He was on his third cop and third explanation and he was starting to feel like a trick pony. But the Rite Shop already looked like a circus. The thief had been trucked away by ambulance but the store was crowded. Along with two cruisers' worth of police there was Fil's stubby wife in her nightgown, and Gran in her lucky bingo shirt. She'd been killing time, too. Outside, neighbours peered in through the glass window or huddled around the doorway.

Rhan led the officer around behind the shelves, to Stormers.

"I was playing here," he said. "When I look up, I see what's going on. And the guy grabs Fil, so I pull a can — " he took one off the shelf and faked the pitch, " — and I nail him."

The constable looked at the shelf that Rhan had to tiptoe to see over, then at the forty feet across to the store's front counter.

"Don't take this personally," he said in a low voice, "but you're not tall enough to make that shot."

"I know. I had to jump."

"You *jumped* and still hit him?"

"Yeah."

The officer's eyes were wide. "You play a lot of ball, son?"

"No. None." A nudge from inside. "And I can't lift 160 pounds, either," he said under his breath.

"What?"

"Never mind," Rhan said.

The cop was still looking at him. "Think you could do it again?"

If everything was the same, Rhan thought. If I didn't think about it, if somebody needed me to do it, if I was just madder than I was afraid.

He set the can on the shelf. "No," he said with a grin.

"Well, when you're looking for an agent, give me a call," the cop said, shaking his head.

The circus was beginning to break up. By the till, Gran was giving their new address to another constable. Fil cornered Rhan and began pumping his hand.

"We'll miss you. My kid's dentist will miss you." He stepped in suddenly close. "Hey, you remember my advice?"

"Women are trouble."

Fil nodded solemnly. "Women are trouble," he repeated.

Then Gran was at Rhan's elbow. "Time to get rolling," she said.

Rhan glanced at Stormers and felt a pang. He'd been so close! But this sacrifice, he knew, had been for a worthy cause.

Outside on the sidewalk, Gran grabbed him suddenly around the neck and kissed the top of his head.

"Hey!" Rhan wriggled away, the heat rushing to his cheeks. "You can't do that. I'm almost legal, you know."

"Legal to what?"

"Well, to drive."

"You mean I have to stop kissing you once you're old enough to drive?"

Rhan smirked. "Yeah."

Gran checked her watch. "I've still got an hour. C'mere, you."

She chased him, laughing, across the street.

Inside, she phoned for a cab.

"He'll be here in ten," she said. "Check around, make sure you're not forgetting anything. I think they start bulldozing on Thursday." Her voice had a faint echo. "You know, this is the first time I ever left a place that I didn't have to clean." She paused. "Feels pretty damn good, actually."

The suite was almost empty. Their own suitcases and few boxes were in the middle of the living-room, but the landlord had sent a truck early in the afternoon to gather up any salvageable furniture. All that was left were odds and ends and junk.

Most of it was in his room. The bulk of the left-behind, not-worth-keeping stuff was his. But that was all right. He was ready for new stuff.

Rhan's heart was running. All day he'd avoided being alone, knowing what he'd think, knowing what he'd feel. And even now the tug was like a pull to the window, as if he could look out and she would be there.

He knew the knight had a problem with people, living and otherwise. He had a problem with helping that spilled over into rearranging.

But he also had something else. Ever since the Rite Shop, and the moment the can had left his hand, he'd been certain. There was a Magic Marker on the floor and he picked it up. And on the flat, white wall he wrote it in letters twelve inches high.

RanVan lives.

He took a breath. Thursday it would be gone,

along with everything else here. But Darryl had been right. It *was* in his head — it was in his blood and his body and his bones. And no matter what happened now, the thing was ignited. This comet in his hand.

The blast of a horn made him jump. He dropped the marker.

"Okay!" Gran called from the other room. "Giddyup, go!"

Rhan hurried out and burst into laughter. Gran had somehow rescued his cowboy hat from the garbage, and now she was wearing it, plastic whistle and all.

"That's great!" he said.

"You get better respect in a hat," she explained, her eyes twinkling.

But not from the cabbie. They wound up loading the trunk themselves, and Gran slammed it shut as loud as she could.

"Well, I guess that's it," she said, glancing around. "Hey, your light's still on."

Rhan looked back over his shoulder. The suite was dark except for his own window, glowing like neon in the night.

"Yeah, it sure is," he said. He grinned at her and snatched the hat off her head.

Gran smiled. "To the bus depot, James," she cried, swinging into the cab. "And don't spare the horses!"

And Rhan blew the whistle with all his might.

EXIT 1st LEVEL

Coming soon

A Worthy Opponent
RanVan 2nd Level

In Thunder Bay Rhan and his grandmother move in with cousin Zoe, the owner of a shabby motel called the Trail's End. The small paper-mill city is a far cry from Vancouver, but it's full of possibilities for a young knight determined to finish his training. Rhan faces a new school, a new video game and a job — pumping gas nights and weekends. He's drawn to the gas-station owner's daughter, Kate, and to her warm family.

But the game that he's chosen at the local arcade is the territory of the Iceman, an adversary who is more than a match for RanVan's own special talents.